Hob Hurst's Legacy

Ophelia Finsen

The Yorkshire Saga
Hob Hurst's House
Hob Hurst's Daughter

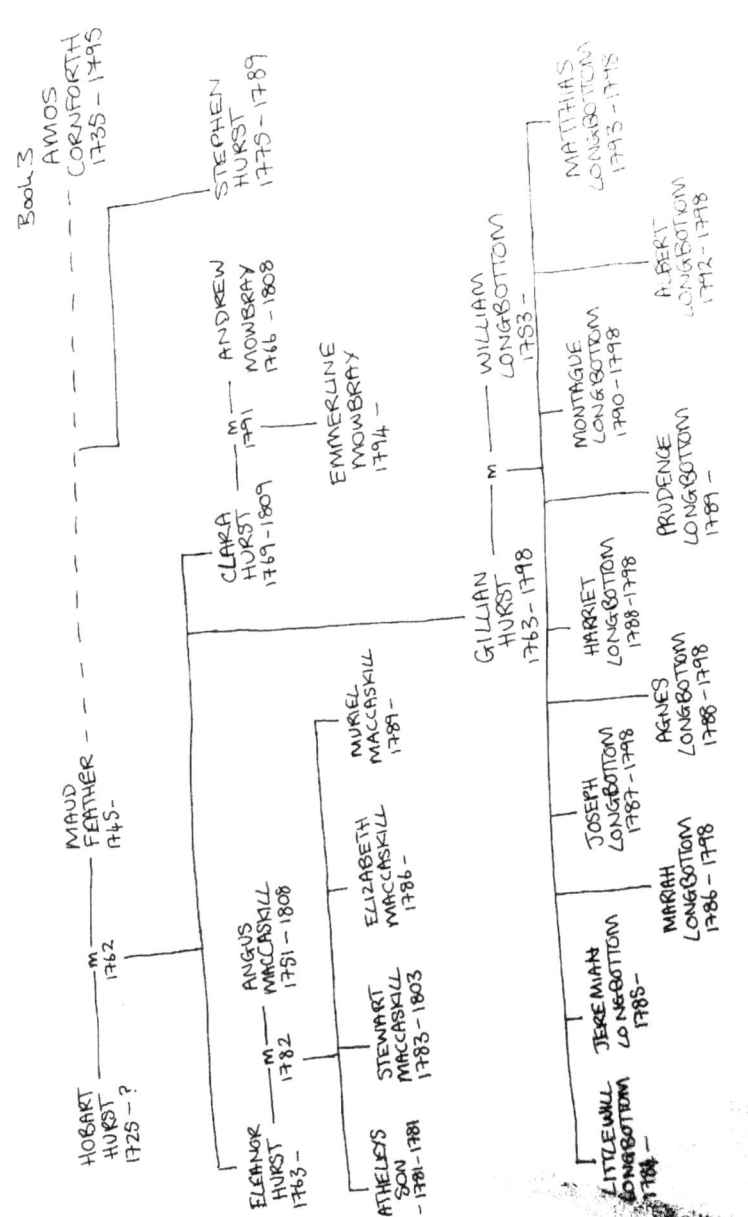

The snow fell in endless sheets. As great flowing rows of laundry waving on steadfast washing lines, battalions of flakes swept across the landscape. There was no sunshine for drying, only the repetitive view of darkening white. It was endless; one could be forgiven for believing existence itself had been swallowed up by this colourless storm. If one did not have the depth of fresh snow piled around the ankles as assurance of the location of solid ground, it would be impossible to say which way up anything was. Visibility was so low that one could lose a hand on an outstretched arm. The wind came with the snow, pummelling great drifts against walls, filling up dips in the land, turning great hummocks of heather into insurmountable mountains. Not that this wintertime landscape could be seen at any great distance. Night deepened the sense of utter isolation, as if the very fabric of the world had disappeared. The temperature dropped and only idiots and the soon-to-be dead were out roaming these heights on such a night.

A figure was struggling through the snow, wading through drifts that held fast at knee-height. The indistinguishable figure was a muddle of hats and coats and cloaks, a bag possibly bulking out the human shape into something more unearthly. The head was down, so that the hat took the brunt of the snow. Onwards forward, blind to everything. The stranger unexpectedly jolted down as if crouching to the knee to pray to the Almighty. The ground had suddenly fallen with a slight ditch and the figure went neatly through extra inches of snow. Cursing, the figure struggled back onto the road, anger superseding the surprising calm that had persevered thus far. Crossing over the track at an angle, the figure walked into a stone wall. A yell erupted, immediately scooped up by the wind and carried across the howling moorland. Hands grasped at the rocks on top of the drystone wall, numb fingers in wet gloves brushing away the snow. It was a well formed wall. Was luck so kind as to have brought up a property wall?

The wretched creature followed the boundary, a blanket of snow forming once again over the shoulders. A break in the wall marked a path, held open with a gate neglected to be shut and now propped open by the snow. As the path proceeded the snow level dropped in equal measure to the wind died off. A building ahead gave shelter. Legs felt the release from wading against snow. The stranger picked up speed and was almost at full sprint when they slammed into the door. Human habitation. The warmth from inside was humming against the door. Fists were hammering against the wood. No human could leave another being out on a night like this.

Yet it was a good couple of minutes before the begrudging sound of locks being drawn was heard. A creak started as the wood was pulled back, slowly, and a voice started to question who was there. As if they could stand and have a conversation at the chink of an open door. The figure was leaning heavily against the door and at the judder of movement, pushed against the entrance, tumbling through into the building, a snow-spilling shivering mass of wet cloth.

"You can't come in here." A young woman, barely twenty and with a look and shadows under her eyes that suggested she did not sleep, leapt back out of the way. She noted with horror the mounds of snow that came in with the stranger. It would soon melt and become her problem. Why did this traveller have to pick their farmhouse? They never got visitors. Who would want to be here? Not even the people who considered this place their abode.

For a moment she wondered about flinging herself out into the storm, hoping for the mercy of nature, but found she was too cowardly, and pushed the door back in its place.

"I hope you told that fool to get away," a deep voice rumbled from within the house.

The young woman glanced to the passageway where light and warmth glowed from the kitchen doorway. She looked back at the stranger. "You should not have come here, sir," she said hoarsely. "We don't entertain strangers."

"You'd send another human being back out in that? What kind of people are you?"

Her eyes widened. She had assumed it was a man, surely only a man would have the strength to have gotten any distance in a storm. Certainly only a man would have been stupid enough, but she was quite sure it had been a woman's voice that had spoken. In a swirl of wet, heavy snow, a shawl and scarf were swept circular fashion from the stranger's head. This action revealed a head in a hat, and a heavy drover's coat over shoulders. Bright eyes shone out from the shadows. It was a woman.

"Come, if you have anything about you, you'll invite me to the fireside. I cannot feel my fingers."

The woman narrowed her eyes. She had no favours in her heart, for life had not been kind, and she would take a beating for letting this woman in. "I told you, you're not welcome."

"Temperance, you're not talking to that fool?"

"A body would die out there in a storm like that. I'll invite myself in." The woman pushed past Temperance and headed in the direction of the fire warmth and the angry male voice.

As the stranger appeared in the doorway, a broad shouldered and angry man, almost more animal than human, jolted up from his place at the table. He was bred of a dark, angry place. Affronted that a stranger should step over his threshold.

"Who the devil are you, man, to enter my house without invitation?"

The woman took off her hat and bowed in greeting. She noted with amusement the reaction to her sex. As well as the unwelcoming beast, there was a lad in his twenties whittling at a stick. He hunched at the end of the table like a dog that was expecting a clip about the ears as the clock would strike nine. Strange for he must have been the same size at the elder man in stature. There was a middle aged woman stirring something at the range who was less cowed than the youngsters and smiled slyly before looking back to her stew.

The man thumped his fist on the table. "What young idiot would be abroad on a night like this?"

"It's been some time since I was called young, but I will accept the compliment. And as the door was opened, I assumed it to be an invitation. On a night like this, any human habitation could hardly turn away a soul in need."

The man, bristling but calming into gruff curiosity, narrowed his eyes. "Who said this was a human habitation?"

The woman at the stew gave a short 'ha'; Temperance, cowering behind the stranger, pursed her lips together and almost made a comment about the devils she lived with but thought better of her cheek before her tongue had chance to act.

The stranger gave the occupants of the room another look. She considered the long deep shadows thrown out from the fire. The flickering light cast out, almost alive in its own right. The master of the house had unruly dark hair, unkempt and a touch too long, giving him a hairy, animalistic look. His brow loomed over his eyes, almost catching them right back into shadow were it not for the slightly evil glint that glittered there.

"You certainly all have the look of humans," the woman said. "But many take on that guise. Perhaps I have come to the abode of hobgoblins?"

Temperance's eyes widened in horror. What an ungodly thing to joke about.

The older woman laughed. "Most of us here are normal common folk. Not so sure about the master of the house."

There was amusement on his face. "You'd insult a potential host?"

"So there is the potential for me to sit out the night? In that case, might I dry my hat and scarves by the fire?"

"Why would you come here on such a devil of a night?"

"To be truthful, I am not sure where here is," the stranger confessed as she passed her outdoor clothes to the housekeeper. "I know I am somewhere on the high moors. I was heading for Haworth, but really I ought to have reached it by now. The snow grew worse than I had expected. I lost my bearings. I have some experience of walking through blizzards and know the area reasonably well..."

"But you're not a local. I can hear it in your voice."

"Not born and bred but I own property."

"A woman in a drover's coat who owns property." The man watched her as she bent forward to warm her hands at the fire. One would assume a young person would be the only type to walk out on such a night and reach anywhere. This kind of weather required endurance and energy. But this was no spring chicken. Now that he could look more closely, he could see the abundance of white strands mixed up in her dark hair. The wrinkles at her eyes. The creases on her brow that would not smooth out. "I've heard about you. A Scot, yes?"

"Only through marriage."

"I thought you were a widow."

"One needs to marry in order to become a widow."

The farm lad stopped whittling, his curiosity getting the better of him. "Who is she?"

"None of your damned business."

The woman smiled at him. "Mrs MacCaskill. I live above Haworth, on the hills."

"Those aren't hills. Not like up here."

"Mrs Eleanor MacCaskill?" the housekeeper asked. "I know the woman who helps at your house. Good honest woman. I've heard of you as well. Bit of an eccentric, folks say. Always roaming about."

"Not always, but I'm heading back home now."

"You've picked a good night for it."

"Tell me, how many miles am I from Haworth?"

"As the crow flies, seven."

"Seven?" Eleanor almost shrieked. "Then I have taken a very long detour. Where have I found myself?"

"Top of the world here, Madam," the housekeeper said.

"You're at Top Hail," the man informed her.

"Top Hail," Eleanor repeated the name, careful to keep the surprise and slight horror out of her voice. She'd vaguely heard of the place, a little local gossip here and there, whispered comments and knowing looks. Her mother, who had grown up in the area, would only say there were some bad folk came from up there, and went silent on the subject after that. People tended to shake their heads and say no more. A long time ago the farm had been reasonably successful, given the remote setting and the height. There had been sheep and some crops, and a respectable little handloom business. Twin brothers had run the property, but some disagreement, or illness, or perhaps it had been one of the wives – folks couldn't agree and it had been so many years that the particulars had misted up in local folklore – and the farm had been split into two, a Top and a Bottom. The brothers were long dead, but one of the sons, an angry devil of a man with a wild look known as Horace Denver, owned the Top Farm. His wife was dead and he did not take kindly to outside influences. There had been a number of children but no one was sure how many were still alive. A housekeeper, Netty Duncombe, actually went up to the farm voluntarily to keep house. She was paid, probably not that well, but somehow didn't mind the atmosphere or the isolation, and was tolerated by the master who was said to have a dreadful temper.

"Your mother is Maud Cornforth."

"That she is."

"Didn't she used to be Maud Feather?"

"Yes," Eleanor replied slowly. The Denvers were a curiosity. A family that had not been seen in the little town of Haworth for years. Who shunned other people and were almost a legend in themselves, to the point some Haworth youngsters were not quite sure if they truly existed. Angry, bitter hermits who would have nothing to do with the world. Yet he was very well informed on her own pedigree. She watched him, and would not turn her gaze away although he stared at her with that very intention. There was something almost resembling recognition there. She did not understand. Yet he seemed to be relenting, as if to say, they couldn't throw her back out into the night.

"Mrs MacCaskill, how will you be paying us for this hospitality this night?"

Eleanor almost laughed in his face. This was hardly the definition of hospitality. Yet the stew smelled good and she had no intention of going back out into the storm. Slipping out of her husband's old drover's coat, she revealed a bag tied about her person. "I'll sing for my supper, in a way, if it suits you." She opened the bag and took out her fiddle, wrapped with care in its own blankets. Music was always with her, wherever she did go.

The two youngsters looked greedily on the violin. They did not get to hear music much up this way. There wasn't much in any kind of entertainment or joy. Were they to be blessed this night or would the suggestion be shouted out to the devil as most things were?

Horace merely grunted and sat back down in his seat. Eleanor assumed that was the best she was going to get and set the fiddle to her shoulder. She watched the firelight shadows dance across the stone walls, and just the right tune came to mind.

Eleanor stood on the threshold and felt the crisp sharp bite of frozen winter air at the back of her throat. She gazed across the brilliant white, shadowed in blues. The snow was fine and of unknown depths, flung out as far as she could see. The soft, soundless layers met with the horizon of the high moorlands. The air was so still and chilled as if caught in the pure chink of a glass. She had come further upland than she had intended when crossing country. She'd walked that route countless times and it was the first time she'd been waylaid to such a degree. At least it was all level walking or downhill from here. She would have to get herself across to Top Withins and from there follow the track down the South Dean Beck towards Haworth. Their home was just to the west of the little West Yorkshire town, and sitting on higher ground, perching just out of reach of all that went on.

It looked like an endless winter waste ground, every direction identical. It would have been overwhelming to many, especially in the conditions. At least it was not snowing, so one might see where one was putting the next foot. But a flowing covering of snow hid the dips and trenches. She was used to long distance walking, and the high level landscape having grown up on her own moors, much further east of here. She was in her early fifties and such walking took more out of her than it had done in the past. Still, Eleanor repeated, she was in her fifties and still undertaking such walks. She wasn't retiring into her wrinkles on a lounge chair at home, bemoaning the chills and the lack of respect from the youth. Sighing and paining, doing nothing, thinking less and surrendering to her dotage. Either that or she might already be dead, from childbearing and related ailments, or, had she been poor, a short, overworked life in the mills followed by a coughing, skeletal death at the end. All things considered, she was rather blessed.

"I'm told I'm to walk you back."

The lad neither looked nor sounded pleased with the prospect.

"If you could just point me in the direction of Top Withins."

He looked surly. "There's bogs and dips and the likes. You'll fall in a drift and die."

Eleanor grimaced as she wrapped the scarf around her neck and the back of her head. That vote of confidence instilled much self assurance. It was daylight, there was no snow falling and it wasn't the first time she'd been out on moorland in winter. She'd walked most of the country with her droving husband before he'd passed away, and had learned how to look after herself in all terrains and weathers. He was gone now, but his old droving coat, a little long on her, kept her warm and waterproof. She walked down what she assumed was the garden path to the gap in the stone wall, her feet crunching through the soft depths of virgin snow. Fresh, frozen flakes pressed against the fabrics of her long skirts, the long leather boots underneath giving protection to her shins.

"Just you wait there, Abraham Denver."

Eleanor turned to see the young woman, Temperance, appear in the door. She pushed past the lad – was he brother, cousin or something else she was not sure, only that they did not seem very keen on one another – and bustled through the snow towards their overnight guest. Out in the bright light and set against this snow background, the young woman looked even more wan and drained than before. She came right up to Eleanor, so close as if to push Eleanor back on her rear into the snow, but stopped short. Keeping her back straight to Abraham, she slipped some folded grubby papers out of her apron and pressed them onto Eleanor.

"You're from Haworth, you're going there now," she almost whispered, not looking Eleanor in the eye.

"What you up to, Temperance?"

"Won't you deliver this for me? The address is just there."

"Temperance?" the lad started to stride towards the women.

Eleanor's eyes flicked up towards the lad as she took the papers, no time to check the name and wonder if there was anything untoward about it, and put them inside her coat.

"I'm just giving her a bit of bread for her walk," Temperance announced, stepping back to publically pass Eleanor a crust end of bread, roughly cut as if someone had been at it with a tree saw.

"Get your lazy self back in that kitchen, damned girl!" Horace Denver yelled from the doorway. "Mrs MacCaskill needs to be on her way. I'll have no idling and chatting."

He ducked back into the shadows and Eleanor observed the house. Despite the bright snow it was still dark and unwelcoming. This high up and isolated, it would take the brunt of the weather; the winds would show no mercy. It had made its residents brutal, almost soulless. She could feel more than see Horace scowling at her from the half open door. Even the house seemed to glare, with only narrow windows to keep in its secrets and keep out the winds and the rest of the world.

"I'll get back, there's nothing undone." Temperance snapped. As she turned she gave Eleanor a secret, pleading glance, so quickly done it was almost missed, before she was dragging her skirts back through the snow to the house.

"Be off with you," Horace called to the lad. "You've chores waiting. Get rid of that damned woman and be back here before noon."

Abraham spat in the snow. Eleanor pushed her hat deeper on her head. "We'd best get started."

Eleanor MacCaskill lived in a solid two storey cottage built of dense, wind-repelling rock. It was sited just west of Haworth, up on the rise with a view down the slopes through the entirety of the little town. She had purchased the property a number of years ago as a comfortable home for her ageing mother. Maud had grown up in Haworth, left when she was eighteen and had only returned to marry her second husband, now deceased, when she was much older. She was content to be back at the moors of her childhood.

The house had also served of one of several bases for Eleanor, but with time her roaming had reduced and she found herself more permanently settled in Haworth. She lived with her mother, Maud, and her youngest daughter, Muriel and they managed well enough. There was a housekeeper who came up to help with cooking, chores and cleaning six days a week and provided a little company for Maud. Maud's walking was very restricted now and she rarely left the house. Eleanor and Muriel liked it well enough, and kept themselves busy, but neither were local. They longed for the sea of the East Coast. Haworth was up in the hills, a long way in land, perhaps as far in land as one could get on this island nation. It was as close to the west as it was to the east.

It was with a sense of relief when Eleanor caught sight of the top of the roof, and the smoke coming from the chimney. Home. She had travelled the country and slept in all kinds of beds, but there had only ever been three places she had ever considered home. Home was where the people you treasured were. That ought to be all that mattered although she still did miss the sea sometimes. Yet despite the chills and the winds, the three generations were quite secure in this little house.

Eleanor had left the lad, or rather he'd left her with the slightest of goodbyes as soon as the Top Withins farmhouse had been in sight. From then on she had walked on her own. She hadn't minded the solitude for those hours, but now that she was within sight of home, she felt ready for company and a bit of conversation. She hurried down the final slope, pushing up fine sprays of snow as her giddy feet skidded through drifts and stumbled up to the door. Great clumps of white snow slopped off her coat and skirt tails with every heavy step.

A greeting of homely civilisation met her like an airlock between the bitter winter and the comfort of a fire as she wrenched open the door. The door swung heavily shut behind her, and almost immediately the crusted layers of snow on her clothes, frozen through the weaves of cloth, began to melt. Anne Thwaite, their shapeless, faithful and good natured housekeeper stuck her head through the kitchen doorway at the back. She looked in consternation for a moment before realising the snow-dipped creature was Eleanor MacCaskill.

"Mrs MacCaskill!" She exclaimed, hurrying down the corridor. "When you didn't come home yesterday I thought maybe common sense had finally caught up with you and you had decided not to walk over the moors. Looking at you I'm not so sure now."

"I walked but I had to take shelter at a farm overnight," Eleanor said as she shrugged out of the drover's coat. "No, don't burden yourself with all this," she added as Anne went to take the outdoor wear from her. "You'll be busy enough in the kitchen."

"And I don't want to busy myself too much cleaning up after all your snow in the hallway, so I'll just take these things now."

"Smells good, whatever you're doing in there. Where is my mother?"

"In the parlour. She was feeling tired so she went through for a rest."

"I'll go see her." Her mother had always liked to help out with the baking and household chores, Maud had been a paid maid until eighteen. It was impossible to get the habit out of her. She had turned seventy this year and was slowing down. Increasingly by the afternoon she would quit the work of her own accord and go to the parlour to rest. Embroidery, knitting, reading and painting were pastimes she'd never been brought up to do, and so, with little entertainment one could enjoy whilst sitting, she tended to doze more often than not.

Eleanor paused in the doorway, regarding her reclining mother. She was slumped in the armchair, her feet up on a little footstool, and snuggled down into a depth of shawls and scarves. Her hair was almost completely white, the trials of life having sucked the colour from her. The early damage to her face, a nasty break in her front jaw from an unsuccessful but vigorous attempt at tooth extraction by a blacksmith, seemed to stand out a little more with every year. Maud thinned and thinned, and looked more the genial old crone.

Eleanor walked in and leant forward, rustling the fire back into action with the metal poker.

Maud shifted in her seat and slowly opened her eyes.

"Good afternoon, mother."

"Eleanor, you're back," she said hoarsely. "What time is it? I was just to rest for five minutes. I left Anne with all that bread..."

"Nothing for you to be worrying about." Eleanor pulled a second armchair closer to the fire so she could sit down opposite her mother. "Is Muriel back?"

"No." Maud yawned and shifted position in the chair to sit a little more erect. "Still at Halifax. Still working hard at her art."

"I'm still not sure that her heart is in it. She does it because she feels she ought than that she wants to."

"No more or less than most folk." Maud regarded her daughter. It was so strange to see this middle aged woman before her, whom she could still remember as a little girl running off across heather moorland, ragdolls in hand. "You did not try to travel last night in the storm, I'm glad."

"Well, I did," Eleanor admitted. "I got a little lost and had to take shelter in a farmhouse. I'd been heading for Top Withins but ended up a few miles south, at a place, what was it called? High Hail or some such thing."

"Top Hail Farm," Maud quickly corrected her.

"They were strange folk there. I think they would have happily watched me perish in the snow. A lucky thing I am too forward for my own good and stepped inside as soon as they opened the door."

"Samuel Denver wouldn't do such a thing."

Eleanor raised her eyebrows, a little surprised by how vehement Maud sounded. "Well, I don't know about Samuel; I didn't see or hear of one there. There was a dark and gruff man full of spite and swearing, Horace he was called. And two young folk, Temperance and Abraham."

"I wouldn't know them. But what about Samuel, where was he?"

"I don't know, I haven't the faintest idea who he is."

"He was always good to me, Samuel, when I was working up at the house," Maud said vaguely.

"He was someone you knew in Haworth before you moved to Commondale?"

Maud looked confused.

"You don't talk much about those days."

"They're all dead now of course," Maud said as if she was only just realising it. "You were at Top Hail?" she looked sharply at Eleanor. "Bad folk come from there. You shouldn't have gone there."

"I didn't go on purpose. I lost my way in the storm and had to take shelter where I could. Besides, I don't think they're all bad," she added, thinking back to the girl, Temperance, and the imploring look as she furtively passed across the letter. "Perhaps just disadvantaged from being so isolated."

"That's your good rock steady belief in the Christian goodness of all, Gillian." Maud said. "But some folk are nothing more than the devil's work."

An unsettled stillness moved between them. Eleanor watched as Maud gazed into the flames. She'd called her daughter Gillian a couple of times in the last few months. A slip of the tongue she'd not even noticed. Easily done when one was tired or distracted, yet the only time prior she had made the error had been back at the farm in Commondale when Eleanor and Gillian had been young girls and Maud had been at her wits end. They had been twin sisters, but Gillian had been dead these past fifteen years. Eleanor lowered her eyes. They had not been close in the last years of Gillian's life; indeed it had been strained, for they were very different personalities. But twins have a close bond and her sister's death had left a slice of a wound in her being that would never heal up.

Maud's eyes were starting to droop again.

"I think I'll go see what Anne has planned for supper," Eleanor announced, standing up abruptly from her chair. Maud merely nodded at the suggestion and slipped back into sleep. The crackle of the fire and warm flickering glow of the flames accompanied her slumber as Eleanor left her and stalked down to the kitchen.

The letter waited on the mantelpiece for two days. Eleanor had caught a mild chill and stayed in bed the day after her winter trek. When she finally roused herself and declared that she would live yet, she spent a great deal of time in the parlour, gazing at the letter and wondering what was inside. It was none of her business and she had promised, although in not so many words, to deliver it. Yet she knew the address would take her to a depressing part of Haworth. What would a girl, locked away in a remote farmhouse high on the moors, be doing writing to someone in the deepest part of Haworth. A place where people worked hard, lived in cramped, coughing conditions and died young. If Eleanor had lived there she would be dead twice over by now. What on earth did

Temperance Denver have to say, and to say secretly to people she couldn't have possibly met?

The next morning Eleanor decided to be proactive. It was Sunday, and chances were the family would not be working, so she would be able to deliver the letter. She dressed, breakfasted, and with a glance out of the window selected sturdy boots. It had warmed up and was no longer snowing, but what had fallen had turned to a dirty, slippery slop of slush. The road down into the heart of Haworth was steep and Eleanor did not care to break her ankles today.

She left the house and headed down the track towards the edge of the little town. Here cottages clustered at the head of the main street. Along with the standard buildings stood the parochial house and the church of St Michael's and All Angels. The morning service was already over and crowds dispersed, but the reverend Mr Charnock was still loitering at the gates in case there was one more soul to speak to. Eleanor inwardly winced. She had been allotted the space of outsider-eccentric and got away with a certain amount of mischief, including the old sin of being a haphazard and infrequent attendee of church. It was something Mr Charnock would comment upon whenever chance occurred. He was about the same age as Eleanor, but time had taken him quicker, and was far rounder than his youth, sagged with responsibility and the sadness of so many hopeless souls in his flock. Muttonchop whiskers caught the damp chill in the air, almost sensing a sinner approach. Pouched eyes latched onto Eleanor's spritely form.

"Good Morrow to you, Mrs MacCaskill," he called, stepping out to intercept her. "You were missed in church. I see you must have overslept."

She smiled tightly and did not slow in her walking. "Mr Charnock," she nodded to him. "You must excuse me; I am on a mission this morning."

"Aren't we all."

Away into the town, the road steeply descended, the air quality dropping as the smog from the mills pooled up around alleyways and dingy doorways. Slops were thrown out of windows and doorways into the street. At least in winter the smell was beaten into submission by the chill. The solid remains froze so as not to be tramped up and down in the street. In the summer the entire area fair stank to make one beyond nauseous. Families existed crammed into single rooms, barely there for they worked such long hours and from such a young age. Damp washing hung out despite the chill in the hope that the winter sun might help a little, or at worse it was out of the room for a few hours. She had to ask a few people before she located the correct wynd, and found the door of the Heatons. A woman was busy just inside the doorway peeling potatoes. She was thin and looked old but Eleanor doubted she was much older than her own daughters. Behind her a couple of young children slumbered in a shared bed, awake but too weary to play.

"Excuse me, I'm looking for Daniel Heaton."

The woman's eyes narrowed as she took in Eleanor. "Who are you?"

"My name is Mrs MacCaskill."

"And why would you be wanting a Daniel Heaton?"

"Have I come to the right place? I believe this is the home of the Heaton family."

"Home would be stretching it," the woman muttered. "What are you about? Well dressed as you are, you don't live down here. What is it? Sending a woman out to collect money, and on a Sabbath as well? You ought to be ashamed..."

"I am not here to demand money, merely to pass a message on to Daniel Heaton."

"We don't need any more messages down here."

"If you could just..."

"Ma, what is all this going on?" A young man of about twenty appeared. Smart as he could afford, but his clothes were shabby and had been repaired one too many times. He wore fingerless woollen gloves to try and protect his hands. Tools of his trade as a trainee stone mason. "Did I hear my name?"

"He doesn't live here no more," the woman flashed Eleanor a look. "You leave him out of whatever mischief you've brought. We saved to get him that apprenticeship..."

"I promise you, I am not here to take anything. Are you Daniel Heaton?"

"I am."

"Then this is for you." She handed across the letter. "That is all I came to do, and now my errand is complete."

He looked at the letter, and in particular the handwriting, lost in thoughtful contemplation for a moment before looking at Eleanor. "How did you come by this?"

"I was given it for delivery."

"By?"

"By someone at Hail Top Farm."

"Oh my sweet," he burst out, ripping open the letter and unfolding the paper. "Finally a response."

The woman, presumably the mother of all, curled her lip. "Nothing but bad uns. It'll bring nowt but misery."

He gleefully waved the letter at her. "She has accepted me!"

"Aye, but has the father? I think not."

"It does not matter, she is old enough. She is coming. She is coming soon. There is too much to organise. I must go to the church and see the reverend this instance." He marched off up the alleyway, before turning and hurrying back to Eleanor. "I have not thanked you," he said, shaking her by the hand as if they were old reunited fellows. "Thank you. You have brought the news that my life has been waiting for. I did not catch your name?"

"Mrs MacCaskill. And it was no trouble."

"I cannot imagine for the life of me why you would have been up at that god forsaken place, but I am glad you were. You must excuse me, I have much to arrange."

And with that he was scampering off down the narrow alleyway again, full of great cheer. The woman, the matriarch Mrs Heaton, scowled as if she foresaw bad things to come. A baby within started to cry and with a weary drop of her shoulders she accepted her moment of peace was finished. She looked Eleanor straight in the eye, saying nothing, then retreated inside and shut the door in Eleanor's face.

Maskew's Jewellers in Halifax was a respectable family business well known to the locals. The shop building stood very close to the Piece Hall, where cloth was traded and fortunes made. It was money that could then be spent on adornments, keepsakes and future family heirlooms.

The owners were third generation Maskews and all looked promising that at least one of the fourth generation would take up the family business as the elders grew too weary. Beyond the neat, dignified shop facade was a quiet, reflective showroom, suggesting contemplation on one worthy purchase that would be treasured a lifetime. These weren't trinkets to be replaced every other week. The room was lined with glass cabinets of mahogany frames displaying the latest wares and fashions to adorn the local, wealthier women of West Yorkshire. A quiet feel of study, almost nearing the focus of a library pervaded the very building.

A tinkling bell interrupted the sense of musing as Eleanor MacCaskill pushed open the door. She paused on the threshold, noting the current lack of custom. She was glad that she had decided to call at this hour. Mr Maskew was at the far end of the room busy over a book of accounts. To the right Mrs Maskew was assisting a young lady with a purchase. She did not look utterly convinced at the woman's direction of interest, with a worry that neared distress for wellbeing and health. She did not dare physically take the woman's arm and pull her away, but she was very near to it. "Those are mourning jewellery."

"Yes, I can see that," the woman said brashly. "It's very intricate how you get the locks of hair in."

"But I thought you said your friend was getting married?"

Eleanor pursed her lips together, thankful she didn't have to get involved in this level of selling. It was bad enough sometimes getting a good price from the traders, low enough so that one might make a reasonable profit without the buyers feeling they were being swindled. But to have to negotiate with the general public, persuade them on style and appropriate nature of items whilst they kept a tight finger lock around their grubby purse strings, that felt like too great a feat.

Mr Maskew looked up over his half moon glasses and caught sight of Eleanor. "Mrs MacCaskill," he exclaimed. "I was hoping we'd see you sometime soon. And here you are."

"And here I am." She walked over to the counter.

"Our workroom is getting low on amber and jet. Not that there is a great call for jet per see, but it does polish up fine and look nice on the mourning jewellery." As well as the shop front,

Maskews also had a workroom of artisans working on the new pieces to be sold.

"I don't have any jet with me today but I can return next week on that account. I was here due to a recent shipment of amber from the Baltic." She shrugged the bag over her head and shoulder and set it upon the counter. Inside there was a piece of soft linen wrapped around raw chunks of amber.

Mr Maskew picked one up, holding it up to the light. "The clarity is very good, although do I see a crack here?"

Eleanor didn't respond. Not only did they both know the quality of her wares, but also that she knew amber better than he did and wouldn't be fooled. They were years into a business arrangement now, but at the start he had been a little bemused by this spritely woman turning up claiming to be a merchant of semi precious stones. A woman who was an independent trader was not known in these parts and he assumed she'd taken it up after a bereavement. He had hoped she would be good for unwittingly low prices. It hadn't worked out that way, although she was fair in her negotiations and with a weary resignation had not taken offence at his assumptions. She wasn't going to change the world by arguing with this man, and in the meantime business needed to be concluded. Halifax might be surprised, but the fact of the matter was that Eleanor had come from Whitby, where women working and managing business was more normal. What with the men being out on the ships for months on end, it had all started out of necessity. Someone had to keep the home fires burning.

As they discussed price and the jewellery trade in general, Mrs Maskew lost the attention of her customer completely. The pieces on offer were not sparking an interest, and her ear had been caught by the conversation on the other side of the room. In her long straight skirts and jacket, she had drifted over as if blown by a breeze, and surprised Eleanor as she suddenly appeared by her arm.

"Do beg the intrusion, but did I hear you speaking of Russia?"

Mr Maskew smiled warmly, Eleanor looked a little alarmed at the sudden voice, unexpectedly by her ear. She looked around to see a box-faced young woman in her twenties, somehow extraordinarily confident and uncomfortable with herself at the same time, with forced curls to frame a face that wanted them as little as they wished to be there.

"Baltic amber, Miss Lister," Mr Maskew said. "We have a very reliable supplier in Mrs MacCaskill. Gets it all the way from Russia."

"Well, technically Estonia."

"But them that were annexed by the empire."

"Yes," she admitted. And she'd had to play by Russia's trading game to continue in her work, but the men she dealt with who sailed into Whitby were very proud of their Estonian routes, and would only negotiate in Estonian or English.

"Russia," The woman's eyes lit up. "And you go there to buy amber? I do so wish to go to Russia."

"I'm afraid not, they come to me. I trade out of Whitby."

"Oh," the intensity dropped a little. "But you are meeting with Russians?"

"Estonians."

"But Mrs MacCaskill has an agreement with the Russian queen," Mr Maskew interjected. "Not just anyone can trade with the empire. That's why such traders are worth their weight in gold."

"You have written to the Russian empress?"

Eleanor smiled awkwardly, feeling she could not give this Russia fanatic what she wanted. "I have had paper correspondence with her office. I'm quite sure she doesn't personally sit and write to every request."

"But this is so exciting. And a woman in business."

"Whitby woman are strange, Miss Lister," Mr Maskew chuckled. "Why, they're almost like men!" His wife flashed him a glare and he coughed on his sudden embarrassment. There were rumours about this resident of Shibden Hall, and it wouldn't do to offend a regular client.

"Well, this is refreshing to meet someone with connections out in the world," Miss Lister said.

"Perhaps you would be interested in an amber piece?" Mrs Maskew suggested, trying to lead her customer back into the thought of purchases. "It does glow very warm especially when worn."

"No, I shall have to leave it for today; my head's all a rush with the east now. Mrs MacCaskill, it's been a pleasure." And with that she swiftly shook Eleanor's hand and marched out of the jewellers.

"Well," Mrs Maskew muttered under her breath, smoothing down her skirts to try and rectify all that was wrong with society. She returned to her desk to tidy up the mourning jewellery she'd taken out of the display cabinet.

"You'll be wanting to see Muriel, no doubt."

"If she's available."

"She can take an early lunch."

Muriel was apprenticed to the jewellery makers and was showing an aptitude for the mourning jewellery – fine pieces with small locks of the deceased's hair twisted decoratively inside. Really she was far too old, at twenty six, to be apprenticed, and the family money from Eleanor's trading meant that she didn't need to work. But domesticity at home bored Muriel and she needed to be doing something. Out of a favour to a valued supplier, Maskews had suggested letting Muriel have a go at the jewellery. She had a keen eye, patience and nimble fingers which all helped her progress in the techniques quickly. It was good to be busy and feel useful, for although previously she had read feverishly at home to keep her brain busy whilst she helped with household chores, Muriel was a little socially awkward and did not have the traditional feminine features that would have brought offers of engagement to her door. In fact, she had never received one proposal and as the years went on it looked less and less likely that matrimony would ever be hers. There were many who sighed and shook their heads, for what was the point of a woman's life if not to keep a home and children? It was all very well burying her head in those books, but a woman's head ought not to be too filled with learning. She'd only dream of that which she could not have.

"So you met the infamous Miss Lister?"

"Infamous?" Eleanor raised her eyebrows as she walked with her daughter down the street. "Is she a picky customer? She certainly couldn't make her mind up whilst I was there."

"She's a bit infamous round Halifax. She lives up with her aunt and uncle at Shibden Hall."

"She did strike me as an eccentric. But I don't see that there's anything wrong with that. It's good to have an enquiring mind."

"You always say that, although I don't know what use it is unless one is allowed to put it to its ultimate use." Muriel grumbled.

Eleanor regarded her younger daughter. They did not look alike at all, only in height, which was to say nothing at all. Eleanor's hair, albeit it full of grey now, had been dark, but Muriel had inherited her intense red locks from the Scottish side of the family. She was a slight woman, so built of straight lines and awkward angles that she was like a body that had yet to have its gender added. A somewhat plain face with a tendency to look like a truculent young lad when she was feeling aggrieved.

"Do you not enjoy the apprenticeship?"

"Oh yes, I like it well enough," Muriel sighed.

"And it is something to do. Something more than running the house. I have offered that you can learn the trading from me..."

"I'm not interested in business."

"Muriel, I wish I knew..."

"I read books."

"Novels?"

"No." Muriel rolled her eyes. "Textbooks. Scientific journals. They have talks here in Halifax on all kinds of subjects. I sometimes go. I've even seen Miss Lister at some. Oh, Mamma, they're so interesting and I feel a fire lit within me. I want to learn, really learn. There is so much to scientific discovery."

"Science is a man's realm."

"But you do a man's job."

"There is a precedent for that in Whitby. I..." Eleanor stumbled for words. She did not wish to place restrictions on Muriel, but she could not encourage her in an endeavour she knew would be impossible. "These scientific organisations, universities, they don't admit women. Oh, they might let you attend a talk now and then, but that's all."

"If I could go to university."

"I wish I could help you with that. Had you been born a boy..."

"It's not fair."

"I know. There's a lot in this world that isn't right." They paused in their walk as a line of scruffy dirty small children went running across their way. Probably coming from or going to one of the pits. If one did not have money one ended up with the hard labour, regardless of age.

"Come on," Eleanor sighed, squeezing Muriel's shoulders. "Come with me and I'll buy you a cup of tea and a bun and tell you of all that's been happening in Haworth since you've been gone."

It was strange how a person could crop up in one's intersecting spheres of association. So distant they might never have existed, then suddenly their name was everywhere. Muriel watched Anne Lister talking animatedly to Dr Bernard Hartley, and wondered if she'd realised why she was there at all. Certainly she represented the higher classes, living at Shibden Hall with landed relatives, but she was also known as an eccentric and something of a dinner party entertainment. Viewing the seated figures at the table, Muriel guessed that at least half were here either for the amusement of the 'proper' guests, or merely out of pity.

Muriel was under no illusions as to why she was invited: she was an object of charity. She was quite sure there'd be hysterical laughter should she start on her ideas of what women were capable of and more importantly what she wished to do with her life. Emmerline's poor, deluded cousin. Not that the MacCaskills were really poor, certainly not like the mill workers of Haworth and Halifax. They were in fact more financially set up than a lot of families, even some of the supposed rich at the table tonight. But she knew that Moses Whitfield, Emmerline's ridiculous husband, looked down upon the MacCaskills as the poor relations and as only being 'trade'. Merchants and jewellery makers. Ex farmers. The father had been a drover, by man, that was little better than a tramp, wasn't it? Not really the class one wanted association with. Muriel didn't get many invitations to the grand Whitfield estate between Hebden Bridge and Halifax (far enough out of both to not be bothered by the smog and the suffering of the hobbled workers whose hard work paid for this empire). Every now and then she'd get an invitation to dinner, or to a really big ball, where there were so many that a plain little thing, uncomfortable in a ball gown, would vanish into the wallpaper.

Emmerline meant well, but she was only young, five years Muriel's junior, and had been pushed into this grand role through marriage. It expected more experience than she could give. Although occasionally Muriel would catch glances in the corner of her cousin's eye and wonder what had gone on in her earlier years before they'd first met over very tragic circumstances. Something indefinable suggested that Emmerline could look after herself better than anyone gave her credit for. She'd briefly lived with her grandmother, Maud, when she had become orphaned, but her paternal aunt and husband had swiftly come in, sick with the scent of money and taken over the girl's upbringing, sending her off to private school, managing her allowance, appointing themselves custodians of the fortune. Moses Whitfield had taken over all of that when he had pushed the ring onto Emmerline's finger. And so she had ended up in West Yorkshire, after a schooling that saw her study for a brief time in Yorkshire, before a finishing school in France. She had returned to England to be married off to a rich, up and coming mill and pit owner, Moses Whitfield, who was looking for a pretty and accomplished wife to finish off his collection of money making businesses, grand house and gardens and enviable collection of expensive furniture. They'd only been married a year as yet, but no doubt a fine selection of children would be on the horizon.

Emmerline was a beauty. She had inherited her looks from her mother, who had been an intoxicating angel, as Eleanor had once described her. Soft curls of beautiful blonde hair that glimmered in the candlelight that evening. She was decked out in diamonds and fine silks, which on her appeared as natural as the dew, as if it were the very right of precious stones to sit by her collar bone. She had just taken a sip of her wine and was gazing across the table in something of puzzlement. "Why, Miss Lister," she burst out, "I do believe I've come across you before."

Dr Hartley looked relieved as he was released from Anne's eager questioning. Anne's eyebrows went up. "I'm not sure," she said, leaning forward to give Emmerline's countenance a detailed appraisal. "I've not dined at Wainstan Hall before."

"No, I'm thinking a few years ago. I'm sure I've seen you in York."

"Well, I do have some very good friends there I visit. The Belcombes, perhaps you have..."

"I'm not acquainted with them, but I must have seen you about in town. You have a very familiar face. And yes, I have heard of you. I believe we have attended the same school, Manor House School, yes?"

Anne gave a mock grimace. "Only briefly, a year at most."

"Me too, although I went there later than you. I remember mention that you had been there. It was just a stopping point before I was sent to France for finishing."

There was a pause as if Anne was expected to give her own similar story of expensive boarding schools in Europe but there were none to offer and she merely looked politely interested with nothing more to add.

"Darling girl," Moses Whitfield, the ruddy-cheeked husband, boomed down the table, "Don't bore Miss Lister with your young ladies' education. I'm sure she and no one else has anything to learn from it." He chuckled to himself and looked over at his long term friend, first time diner at Wainstan Hall, William John Scott. In a lower tone he added: "All this nonsense about educating women. Let the poor ones get to work in the mills, the rich ones find a husband and the saucy ones spread..."

"Moses," Emmerline broke in. "I don't think that's quite the subject for the dinner table. There are a number of us ladies present." She glanced across to the other women, a couple of whom were reddening and looking horrified. There were some she needed to worry over like lost kittens, others she was confident would be fine. She knew her cousin Muriel had far too an in depth and analytical understanding of the world to be shocked by such talk, besides, there was her own sister's lifestyle to consider. And Anne Lister, well, she couldn't quite put her finger on it, but felt she'd stand up to the worst of it with the other men.

"Quite right," Moses chortled, picking up his wine glass.

Muriel watched his red, flushed chops knock back the wine. He was drunk and sweaty already. He was a bit too hairy and far too ignorant to be considered either handsome or eligible in Muriel's eyes. All that mattered in Moses' world was money and appearance. If that was what getting married got you, perhaps it was better that she was utterly overlooked.

His friend of many years, who had been out of the country for the last three or four travelling, exploring, exploiting or whatever it was he had been doing, abruptly stood up from the table and clapped his hands together. "Never mind this nonsense as if ladies aren't as interested in learning as us," he said with a twinkle in his eye.

Muriel watched and felt he was mocking them, but Anne Lister raised her glass and spoke her agreement. William John Scott, she thought, you have mischief on your mind tonight.

"I was going to save this for cigars after dinner, on account of sparing our ladies' nerves," he continued, bowing to the couple of blushing women. "But I think you'd all be interested. Perhaps you have heard from my good friend here that I have been away from our green shores these last three years? I was over in the Caribbean attending family business and then I went to South America to explore."

"Travelling," Anne breathed.

"I am a collector of curiosities and I brought one I picked up in South America for Moses to see. You may not credit what it is or that it is real, but I assure you that this is no cloth stitched toy." He fetched a small box from the side of the room and set it on top of his cleared dinner plate on the table. "Please do hold out your hands," he instructed the two women sitting close by. "For this is not something one would pop in the soup dish."

Moses started snorting his amusement at this. Muriel's attention flicked from one man to the other. They both knew what this curiosity was, and it was clearly going to upset or frighten these simple wives. One of the women looked too nervous from not understanding, and kept her hands folded on her lap. The other, the compliant fool, held her silken palms up in complete trust.

William John Scott lifted the item from the box. It appeared to be suspended on a number of long thick strings, with a tan ball shaped object hanging at the end. Before anyone had chance to really examine it, he had swung it around and placed it into the waiting ladies' hands. "I picked this item up in Ecuador."

"What is it?" Anne Lister leaned forward.

"I don't quite know." The cautious lady muttered uncertainly. Her neighbour peered closely and shifted her hands slightly so that the item rolled in position to meet her gaze. She let out a high pitched scream when it looked at her, and William John

Scott had it nimbly out of her hands before she had chance to throw it across the room in disgust. He had paid a good price for this and had transported it back across the seas in tender care.

Moses was laughing so much that he was almost choking on his own breath. The rest of the dinner table was at a loss as to what had happened.

"You'll have to share the joke, old man," Dr Hartley said.

"I cannot see it in definition in this candle light," Anne Lister spoke. "Is it some dried tropical nut?"

This had the two men roaring with laughter. The first woman to touch it was crying at the dinner table.

"Mary, dear," Emmerline spoke. "Do you need to freshen a little?" Her eyes flashed back to her husband. Guests were not to be treated like this. Her husband did not so much as see her.

"Let's pass this to a man of science," William walked around the table and passed it to the doctor. "He should be able to examine the article without screaming."

"What a beastly object," the doctor commented. "I am in two minds as to whether it is real."

"I assure you it is real."

"I have read about these things, but I have never seen one." He shifted in his seat, a little uncomfortable as Anne Lister was almost upon him to catch a glimpse.

"Shrunken heads are a very real thing," William started, with that self-assured tone that announced he knew all that was to be known on the subject. "This is from South America, Ecuador to be exact, a product of the Shuar tribe's head hunting battle trophy rituals."

"A real human head?" Anne questioned as the doctor gave up examining the item in favour of getting the strange woman out of his chair. "It cannot be so, why this is only the size of a man's fist." She looked to the doctor. "I do not know babies; could a baby's head be this small?"

"With that much hair? I think not," William responded.

Anne stared down at the strange little face, with hair like strings a good fifteen centimetres long. It made a convenient way to carry it. The skin was a dark leathery tan and felt dry and thick to the touch. The slits where eyes, nostrils and mouth had once functioned were now stitched closed. It was such a strange face, a macabre toy, it was hard to credit that it had once been alive, and could have been as much a human being as a monkey. "I do not think there is a skull in here," she said as she ran her thumbs over the strange little head's brow. "This is manufactured."

"Manufactured, but of a human head. They slit open the skin and remove the skull before starting..."

"This is too disgusting and unnecessary," One of the wives declared as she abruptly stood up. In deference to drummed-in manners, all the men immediately rose from the table with her. Bloodthirsty stories were one thing, but an Englishman would not forget his table manners. "Come," she took her sobbing friend's hand and they left the room to sit quietly in the sitting room prepared for the ladies after dinner was complete.

There was a pause and William looked about the room to see if anyone else needed to leave. He only considered the women although a couple of the men would have quite happily departed for the smoking room if they would not have looked foolish. Emmerline seemed distant but unbothered; Muriel looked as though she was trying to restrain her curiosity, whereas Anne Lister had forgotten all notions of restraint and appeared ready to see a working example of how a head was shrunken.

"They pack the skin with hot pebbles to shrink it," William offered as a finale.

"And why do such a thing?"

"These heads, well, tsantsas as those who understand the ritual call them," William explained, including himself in the category of expert. "They are a source of pride and honour. It captures a warrior's soul, so it is a powerful item for a tribe to have."

"So these are war trophies?" Anne spoke as she passed the head up to Muriel. She'd noted how Muriel was equally as curious to handle the item, but was trying to look apathetic. She knew that Muriel had an enquiring mind and wasn't shocked by a little blood. She'd seen her at some of the lectures in Halifax, and furtively taking book orders from the booksellers. She'd come across Muriel hunkered down on a stone on a country lane just above Halifax, trying to read in private. It had been a book on human anatomy. It seemed Muriel had read a lot of medical tomes and instructional manuals. Anne wasn't quite sure how she'd managed to get hold of some of them.

"Indeed. They are sacred items."

"Sacred holy items that they are selling to you?"

William smiled dryly. Moses had warned him they'd collected an interesting array of characters for this evening. "Money talks in all cultures, Miss Lister. And those jungle devils want our weapons. I had to part with a very good knife to get that head. But I would not do without it. Everyone else I know has a very fine collection, and I could not return home without some trophies of my own."

"This Shuar tribe, was that the name? Yes? They must be very busy with their wars in that case. If all the explorers need their heads to take home, it must be difficult to supply everyone and keep their own shrines stocked up."

William John Scott shuffled a little awkwardly at Anne's observation. "Those devils breed like rabbits," he muttered vaguely.

Dr Hartley watched Muriel carefully examine the head. "It does not disgust you at all, Miss MacCaskill?"

"No, only wakens my curiosity."

"And what about our hostess?" William whipped the head out of Muriel's hands and marched around the fine dining table to drop it into Emmerline's alabaster fingers.

As the head landed in her hands, Emmerline felt with a jolt a sense of Rotterdam. A warmth spread up through her fingers as she stared at the lifeless, stitched eye slits. This had once been a human being. A full sized head full of emotions and thoughts. How did you come to be beheaded, she wondered. She looked up at William. "Jan Van Willhelm."

"Good gracious," William said. "Do you actually read geographical periodicals? How do you know of old Jan? He's a great trader and explorer," he explained to the rest of the table. "I've met him, in Ecuador in fact. He was there in Guayaquil when I was first arrived. He set off into the jungles on an expedition. I never got chance to meet with him again before I set off for home. It's a shame, because..."

"Mr John Scott," Emmerline interrupted. "I have no idea who he was. You misunderstand me." She held the head a little higher. "This is Jan Van Willhelm."

There was an awkward silence in the room. Anne stared at the hostess as if she was just a little wrong in the mind. Muriel watched her cousin with more curiosity. She always thought Emmerline, through beauty and money, had been underestimated. William looked lost for words. Moses was the first to break the silence with a loud, booming laugh. "Emmerline, you do talk a lot of rot."

"You are confused my dear lady," William added. "These heads are only made from the warriors killed in battle. Why, even the natives have enough respect to know that one can't do such a thing to a white man."

Emmerline looked back to the head. She thought of the tall Dutchman striding through the South American jungle with his paid team of natives and Europeans workers. The raiding party running through the undergrowth, having run out of the old heads, having run out of new heads, having even killed a few of their own children for the stupid white men who didn't realise that it was only the heads of warriors that had any power. They'd buy anything. The stupid white men couldn't tell the difference between a man and a monkey when it was shrunken. But there was a man from London with a box of guns that wanted a box of heads in return and they needed a windfall fast. A lost group of weary travellers, a long way from anywhere was a godsend. The guns would be traded for and there would be a couple of heads to spare. There were shouts and cries as the headhunters leapt from the undergrowth. Confusion and tired limbs, sudden screams and blood spatters. Jan was stumbling in circles, trying to find his porter who carried his rifle, for he had dropped his gun on the steep climb up to this level. Then something heavy and sharp whacked into the back of his neck with a dull thud and he thought no more.

"Perhaps we should put this away," William suggested, feeling unsettled as he took the head from Emmerline's hands. There was an odd glazed look in her eyes. "I did not think it might upset your guests as much as it has."

They passed by a small group of post funeral attendants on the walk home. It was a family group: a mother aged far beyond her biology, a grey husband and a clutter of children. Hard-worked and worn, underfed and undernourished in all ways, yet with a surprising set of mourning clothes. It was probably not the first family burial. The mother was wiping at her eyes, muttering that this was not the first child she had buried, she ought to be better used to it. One of the pale little girls with her tugged at her skirts and asked her mamma if this meant she wouldn't have to go to the mill tomorrow.

As Muriel and Eleanor walked past the group, Eleanor noted Muriel's countenance stiffen.

"Mr Charnock was saying the other day they struggle to fit all the funerals in. Sometimes three a day."

Muriel let out a sigh. "And when did you become such great friends with the preacher?"

Eleanor smiled. She liked to think issues of humanity went beyond the confines of religion. Funerals had not been the motivation for Mr Charnock to join the cloth back in his youth, but they had become a large component of his working day. Naturally he'd wanted to bring some solace to the grieving, for death was a natural part of life, returning to the Lord and the sanctity of heaven. It was just that in Haworth the harsh reality of the everyday was a little more regular than he would have liked.

Usually Eleanor would avoid Mr Charnock, but he'd caught her the other day as yet another funeral had been coming to a close. She had been walking up the steep hill in the direction of home. He had looked a little grey, shaken, as if the constant reminders of man's mortality were eating away at his own allotted life span. His mood was low, even for a man who ought to have steadfast faith that they were all off to a better place to the grace of God. For whatever reason he'd sought Eleanor out, as if she were the professional handing out solace. There'd been no comment on her absence from church on this occasion, merely a search for a sounding board on all that troubled him.

"Anyway, it's shocking that there's never a problem about funding all of these funerals," Muriel muttered.

"For someone who is working in the business of mourning, you surprise me."

"I'm just an apprentice and I'm not sure how long I'll be there. My days are getting monotonous. Mr Maskew let me have these weeks off."

"You certainly get special conditions for an apprentice."

"We all know they've only taken me on as a favour to you." Muriel paused and watched the funeral group reach a crossroad and walk out of sight. "Those people looked as though they were starving, and yet they'll just have paid out for a funeral."

"They all subscribe to burial insurance, you know that."

"Whilst the family starves and the children work like dogs in the mills. It's insane..."

"It's the way things are. If you're poor and you have to work..."

"Oh, I know all that. I've just spent a week with the obscenely rich." Muriel's lip curled. "The rich built on the backs of thousands of human beings treat with contempt."

"Muriel, people will mistake you for one of these agitators," Eleanor warned. In essence she agreed. It was not right how so many slaved for a pittance, lived in their own filth and dragged their own tiny children to the mills to work long shifts. Whilst others profited on a far greater margin than they needed, then had the audacity to look down upon their workers and declare they were of an inferior breed. Was this the peak of humanity? But people's lives were hard everywhere and being angry would not save anyone. It was such an immense problem she doubted a solution was possible. And for the here and now, not everyone could be saved. Perhaps she was too old to believe anything could fundamentally change. "How is your cousin, anyway?"

"Emmerline? Much the same as always. Cheerful. Positive. Full of the good will of mankind. Still married to that swine."

"Muriel!" Eleanor scolded with a smile.

"He looks down at me like a charity case. As if we're the poor relatives."

"Compared to Emmerline's fortune we are."

"We're not inferior to them."

"You won't change minds such as those belonging to Moses Whitfield. He's hardly worth getting upset about."

"His friend was there, some traveller back from the new world. Moses thought it was funny to mock his guests. He had his friend bring out this South American shrunken head, to try and terrify the ladies. Well, it worked with a couple, but I think doing it at their oddities' dinner was a bad move. They had Anne Lister there for goodness sake. She did not recoil at all. I found it a curiosity. I still wonder quite how it was prepared."

"A shrunken head? Is this an animal preparation?"

"It's a human head," Muriel sounded a little exasperated as if her mother knew nothing of the modern world. "But it's been prepared and shrunken to the size of a man's fist. A primitive tribal thing."

"I hope Emmerline brought some order to her dinner table. I can't say I'd ever have wanted to be lady of a grand house, but despite the finishing schools I don't think she's quite comfortable in the role."

"Emmerline was quite odd about it all actually," Muriel reflected. "She gave it a name, the head I mean."

"She'd heard of shrunken heads before? I wouldn't have thought that would turn up in society notes in the papers."

"I mean a name, a person's name. She gave it a Dutchman's name."

"I thought you said it was from South America."

"It was. But Mr John Scott, that's the explorer, he actually knew who she was talking of. Emmerline claimed she'd never heard of him before. I'm sure she was playing a trick back at them."

"Is that what she told you?"

"No, goodness, she hadn't said a thing to me about it. But she sat there at the head of the table with the object in her hands and looked up and spoke this man's name."

They reached the top of the hill and Eleanor paused for a moment. It was always that last steep pull that caught at her lungs, no matter how often she walked it. She stared at Muriel. "She had it in her hands when she spoke the name."

"Yes, I..." Muriel paused. "Why are you looking at me like that?"

"Nothing. No, I just..." Eleanor shrugged it off. She was thinking back to her own childhood. Some of the odd things she had seen. Muriel was very literal, the here and now and the good explanations of science. She wouldn't want to hear about her old mother's reminiscences and superstitions. The stories and folklore that had plagued the family when they'd lived out on the moors towards the east coast.

Muriel scoffed, reading a look in her mother's eyes. "You don't think Emmerline has otherwordly powers?"

"Well, no of course not. I just remember Clara..."

"Her mother?"

"She could be a little strange as a child."

"She must have been a little strange as an adult, given what happened to her. You've never really talked much about growing up on Commondale."

"Not a lot to tell," Eleanor said evasively, her eyes moving across the cobbled street. "Oh look, could there actually be something happier happening at the church. An actual wedding?"

Muriel narrowed her eyes as she looked to the church. "You know that place is part of the problem."

"Sorry?"

"Rainwater falling on there, soaking through the graves and down into the town's drinking water. People are drinking corpse water."

"Muriel!"

The happy event, a small cluster of people complete with beaming bridegroom and nervous bride, came bursting out of the gateway into the churchyard. There was chatter and the laughter of some scruffy children that seemed to make up the wedding party. The priest followed. He was not a man Eleanor recognised. Had something happened to Mr Charnock? He had not looked so well the other day.

"Mrs MacCaskill!" the bridegroom burst out, catching sight of the bystanders. "Won't you come and share our joy? If it wasn't for you, I don't know that we'd be celebrating this happy occasion."

Eleanor squinted, recognising the voice but finding the facial features a little indistinct at this distance. She had been wondering if her sight had been growing a little worse recently, but had not dared mention it to anyone. Muriel would only laugh at her and tell her to get spectacles. What a ridiculous idea, she didn't want those contraptions on her face. But she had to admit the finer details in her vision at a distance were going. It worried her, especially since her close vision had started to blur a few years ago and she was forced to hold letters and papers ever more further away in order to read them.

"Who is it?" Muriel asked.

She had heard the voice before. She looked to the bride, hung on the young man's arm as they came down the steps from the church. She and Muriel walked over to the bridal party and as they came into focus, she saw the mother of the bridegroom's face and remembered the Heaton family. "Mr Heaton," she exclaimed, looking from him to Temperance Heaton, nee Denver, who was looking decidedly happier than she had up at that remote, snow-encrusted farmhouse, the last time they had met. "I see congratulations are in order."

Temperance gave her a timid smile.

"We have just been wed. Mr Redhead managed to fit us in between funerals."

"Mr Redhead? I thought..."

"I'm helping Mr Charnock out temporarily, you understand." The priest stepped up to the group. "He's unwell and needs some days to recuperate. A parish so troubled by mortality is a heavy burden, and Mr Charnock is an old man..."

Old man my foot, Eleanor thought. He's the same age as me.

"Damn you to hell, priest, for this unholy alliance!"

Muriel stifled a laugh, her immediate reaction to such an out of place and melodramatic curse. She turned with the rest of the group to see where the oath had come from. The very blood in Temperance's flesh seemed to flee as it caught sight of the dark browed man. Mr Redhead, albeit helping Mr Charnock with the parish, but clearly unaware of the more complicated characters of the area, stepped forward in a fashion almost as if he believed the man were making a joke and was here to shake hands.

"I don't believe we've been introduced..."

"Cease your babbling, priest," Horace Denver, the pugnacious, bad-tempered and dark-soul hill farmer, brushed the little holy man aside as he stormed to the wedding party. "I did not give my permission for this. I was not consulted."

"I am old enough to make up my own mind," Temperance stuttered.

"Only in years but not in thought, you feeble-headed wench."

Daniel Heaton, new husband full of love and a desire to prove himself, took a step in front of his bride as Horace went as if to slap the girl. "Don't touch my wife, sir. I'll thank you to show some respect."

"Sir!" Horace laughed sourly. "Aye, she's your trouble now, and may a thousand curses and miseries rain down on your house."

"Father!"

"I'm not your father," he growled. "And don't set foot at Hail again. You're not welcome there." He swung around, oblivious to the shocked array of faces. He ignored the children that had started to cry. "And you," he accused, pointing at Eleanor. "I knew you'd bring trouble when you turned up out of that snow storm. I should have thrown you back out to perish in the storm." He stepped closer, a thump of a footstep that visibly had many of them taking a step away. He bore down on Eleanor, who refused to move. In private, later she would admit that she had been quite frightened. She expected to smell the drink on him as he breathed down into her face, but there was no alcohol. This fury was pure bred.

"My, my," she spoke quietly. "Someone does have a temper."

He pointed at her, almost poking her in the eye. "Watch yourself."

"Sir, I must intervene. This is not Christian or gentlemanly."

"I see no gentlemen here," Horace Denver pushed the priest away for the second time as he strode away. "Damnation upon all of you."

Muriel stepped up to her mother and held on to her arm. "Who was that?"

"Horace Denver," Eleanor spoke quietly, conscious of the chatter behind her. Mrs Heaton was shaking her head and predicting no good would come of this. Two of her younger children were crying. Temperance was babbling, a little hysterically if truth be told, and Daniel was trying to calm her. "He farms up at Top Hail. I had to spend the night there when I was caught out in the snowstorm."

"What storm? When?"

"Oh, you were over in Halifax. Never the matter. I got home."

"What kind of people are they? He behaves as though civilisation has done him a great disservice." Muriel shook her head, not expecting an answer.

"I don't know. There's some strange history there." Eleanor watched Horace's retreating figure stride up the hill. He moved at some speed. He was an immense energy, and full of anger. This performance at the church had not been a sudden explosion as it would have been for many. Horace Denver existed at a consistent level of pulsating fury and hate. She wondered how anyone could sustain it so long. "Your grandmother seems to have known some of their ancestors."

"Really?"

"Come now," She twisted in her daughter's grasp and looked to the wedding party. "Our congratulations to you again." She pulled on Muriel's forearm to get her walking. "Let's go home. I've no desire to get embroiled in anymore family dramas."

Emmerline sat primly in the armchair and gazed into the fire. She was in a daze. There were too many voices buzzing through her mind, all clambering for attention. The world owed them an ear, an acknowledgement of their existence and death. Screaming from the abyss for recognition. There were so few could pick up the frequency. When they found someone, by hell they would make sure their story would be heard and heard in full, even if it drove their sounding board to insanity.

Emmerline had come here to escape all the nonsense at home, but she had found no peace. She had been greeted at the door by the housekeeper who had immediately continued in a half spun tirade on the arrogance of Halifax, thinking it could decide over Haworth. Emmerline would have been furious if one of her staff had greeted a visitor in this manner, but her aunt just let it go. In her defence, she did appear to have other troubles. An opinionated housekeeper was such a trifle in comparison. Even so, why did everyone, living and dead assume Emmerline wished to hear their woes?

She could not help herself. She could not be openly rude. Emmerline carried a burden of empathy for her fellow man, and a need to be kind. People looked at her, with her neat waist and pretty blonde hair and judged her to be an angel. Patient. Caring. Eternal. Why could she not tell them to stop? Deep within she knew she had the strength to scream, and she knew that people would back away. But she could not be unkind. Unkind even where self defence demanded it. She should have done something more that morning in the breakfast room, she knew it. If her husband ever found out all the kindness she could summon would not save her. Thank goodness the staff had not been in the room at the time. There was nothing worse than downstairs' gossip.

That dreadful man, friend to her husband and naive explorer of the world, John William Scott, was over for another visit and he had brought that frightful shrunken head with him again. Her husband was fascinated by it and was talking of purchasing one of his own. He wanted a collection in the house, something to showcase his intellectual side. So he trumpeted every morning at breakfast. Then he was called away to an issue at the mill and Emmerline had been left alone with the visitor. The dreadful man had placed his knife, smeared with softened butter, on his plate, and stood up. Such nonsense had spouted forth, how he had fallen in love with her, and he knew she felt the same too. A woman such as she should be adored, a goddess, and with their mutual love, surely they could enjoy a little time whilst her husband was out at the mill.

A nasty little affair in other words. In many ways Emmerline was apathetic to her husband, but her aunt from York had advised her that marriage was a partnership, a wife needed to respect and regard her husband, and it had been a terribly good match. She could simply not have turned Moses Whitfield down. But he was hardly the hero of romantic novels. Neither good nor kind, neither handsome nor dashing. His mistreatment and contempt was not even of the vintage Lord Byron excelled in that had women swooning.

John William Scott was at her side, looking so earnest, and ready to bury himself in her skirts. She'd been so lost in her thoughts that she had not seen him approach. She had jolted up from the breakfast table, knocking her chair back.

"Mr Scott, pray do not be foolish."

He followed her as she backed away, "I am but a fool in love."

She'd gone to push him away, and had frozen for a moment, recalling the face of another young man she'd pushed away many years ago. He had been equally undeserving and she really had not known her strength, but it had been self defence, and...

"My darling!"

She pushed him back with a yelp as he slobbered to her cheek. She should have thrown him out of the house or at the very least told him in no uncertain terms that she was married and he should behave like a gentleman. Instead she merely stared at him in confusion, thinking back to escapades of her youth, before sweeping out of the room.

It was in the small hours of the morning, before the maids were up to light the fires, and after the alcohol had taken effect and the men were asleep that Emmerline had been woken by incessant chattering. A man who would hear his story told. He would not stop talking. She had lit a candle and walked downstairs and into the morning room. There on a polished walnut table sat the box with the shrunken head. Someone had left the lid off and the face lay still. It would have been staring at the ceiling had it still eyes. No movement yet it did not stop for breath. A Dutchman who spoke excellent English and had been double crossed in the jungle. There was a German collecting flowers who had thought he was competition for the orchids, and had arranged for the natives to take his head. It was the Europeans who had struck the fatal blow. And the world believed he was just lost. Lost in the latin jungle. The world didn't know that he had been stabbed. Hacked to pieces. His body fed to pigs, bones taken for holy objects. His head shrunken down to be sold as a trinket to idiot tourists who fancied themselves as great explorers. His family didn't know the truth. She had to get the head back to Holland. She could not tell him that it was not her problem. He would not stop talking.

Emmerline was packed and out of the house at eight in the morning, leaving a note for her husband that she was going to stay with her relatives at Haworth for a few days. She had heard her grandmother was ill. A mere lie, but as it turned out, closer to the truth than she would have liked. Her husband would be explaining to William John Scott how she liked to do her charity work for poor relatives now and then. Her aunt MacCaskill and family lived in very comfortable circumstances. She suspected her aunt actually had the finances for something much grander – not on the scale of Wainstan Hall of course – but preferred the simple comfort they had settled in to.

She glanced up from her cup of tea, returning to present circumstances, and saw her lady's maid grumpily stalk past the open doorway. She had not been pleased at being woken so early with a list of urgent demands. Moses said she ought to fire the insubordinate beast and hire something – something, his actual choice of word – with a little more respect for her betters, but Emmerline could not bring herself to do it. It must be such a dull life having to run around after another with never a day to oneself. And the maid hadn't done anything truly terrible to warrant losing her job. A woman's simple mindedness, Moses had muttered in reference to his wife, but had let it be and not involved himself in her domestic arrangements.

"He said it was a malady of a woman's mind," Muriel was saying as she leaned across to top up Emmerline's cup with tea.

Emmerline glanced to her cousin. She had not been following Muriel's monologue, although the general gist was that there was something wrong with her grandmother, and her aunt had called the doctor out early this morning.

"There is something fundamentally changed with her brain."

"Muriel, you don't know that," Eleanor sighed. "She's old."

"It's as if there are holes in there and memories from one part are pouring into another."

"Is this not just the confusion of age?" Emmerline tried to bring herself back into the present conversation. She spent too much time day dreaming. Even as she said the words, she did not quite believe them. She had briefly seen her grandmother before the old woman had retired to bed, and she looked noticeably aged compared to the last time she had seen her. The woman had been vague and confused. She was sorry to see it, for the woman had been a rock during a sad time in her youth. At one time she had lived with her grandmother after the death of her parents, but it had only been for a few months before her father's sister had appeared to get her into the right kind of schools and company. Her mother's side of the family were viewed as a little eccentric and not the best influence for a young girl who was to become a wealthy heiress. Especially considering the circumstances of her parents' demise, it was deemed sensible to keep her away from anything else felt less than respectable. Of course, now she was married, she had taken up the connection again. Her husband did not seem to mind too much, merely mocking her for "charitable connections".

"The money you paid Dr Gordonstone for his visit was wasted," Muriel continued. "I would wager he's not read so much as half the books on my bookshelf."

Emmerline's brow creased. "Why...?" she started, but Aunt Eleanor was already talking over her.

"Muriel, having read a few textbooks doesn't make you a medical doctor. There's a lot of years study to warrant a qualification." Eleanor put her teacup down rather abruptly in frustration. "Have you not heard the expression that a little knowledge is a dangerous thing?"

Muriel pouted and folded her arms.

"I have had the strangest night, and little sleep," Emmerline started, raising her voice so that she might be heard. "I'm a little lost now. What exactly has been happening here?"

"Grandmother thinks she is seeing a ghost."

"It was just an angry farmer from the hills."

"Even if it was just that beast from the hills, that in itself is bad enough. What right does he have to be stalking our home?"

Mother and daughter were growing exasperated with one another and Emmerline felt none the wiser. "Perhaps you could tell me from the beginning, the events of last night. A fresh view on the matter may help."

Eleanor had been the first to realise something was not quite as it should be. It had been in the deepest night when she'd abruptly woken. There was little sound, only the creaks of a sleeping house and a low level wind outside. Yet she was unsettled, as if being watched. For a minute or two she lay and stared at the blackness of the ceiling. Then she heard her mother talking, and assumed that was what had woken her. She sometimes muttered in her sleep, so this was nothing unusual, yet the direction of sound was wrong. Eleanor sat up. Her mother was talking outside.

She lit the candle at her bedside, and hurried downstairs. The back door was open, the wind rattling the pictures on the wall. Eleanor set the candle on a table and stepped up to the threshold. There was a half moon that glowed against the indigo night. Troubled clouds raced over the skyline. The very air was unsettled. Maud was not far away, loitering in the yard. Shaking in distress. "Why are you here? Why do you come back now after all this time?"

"Mamma?" Eleanor walked out and gently put her hands to Maud's shoulders. "There's no one here."

"He's here. My husband has come back."

"Amos is dead."

She lurched around in Eleanor's grasp. "Your father!" she hissed.

"She meant grandfather?" Emmerline interrupted. "But he died even further back. Before any of us were born," she added, looking to Muriel.

Eleanor glanced at the fireplace.

"She was seeing things," said Muriel.

"Perhaps, but there was someone there."

"What?"

"I didn't want to alarm anyone."

"You're just dreaming," Eleanor told her mother. The wind blew up, thrashing through her hair and flinging it in all directions. "We should go in."

"He's out here!" Maud shrieked.

"Both of your husbands are dead. Please, come back inside. You need to sleep." Maud pulled against her as if she were about to run to the moors, then relented and let Eleanor turn her back to the house. Muriel's figure was back lit by the candle as she hung back in the doorway.

"What's happened?"

"Your grandmother has just had a nightmare. A waking dream." As the two women entered the doorway, Eleanor cast a quick glance over her shoulder and saw a shadowed figure of a man dart away towards a copse of trees.

"She said there's someone here."

Eleanor's stomach tightened. "There's no one here. Would you take her back up to bed? I see her shawl has blown away to the bushes. I'll just go fetch it."

She would have liked to put it down to a confused elderly mind, but she had definitely seen a figure. A real, bodied man or a ghost? Or perhaps something else? Eleanor didn't like to admit to a belief in the supernatural, especially within earshot of her youngest daughter who lofted her beacon of science and sense. But she had travelled a lot and seen too many things not to wonder. There were reasons people held to the old folk traditions. Made certain they kept the little folk on side. Yet why would her mother's first husband turn up after all these years?

"He was only declared dead, wasn't he?" Muriel mused. "I remember. You had to have him legally declared dead because he just disappeared without a trace."

"Mamma always said he was murdered," Emmerline exclaimed then blushed. It didn't do to speak of her mother, a disgraced woman and an embarrassing memory in polite society.

Eleanor waved off her reaction. "Don't redden on your mother's behalf. None of us are responsible for others' actions."

"So was it grandfather?"

"Perhaps he had lost his memory?"

"He'd be very old now."

"You read too many gothic novels, Emmerline," Eleanor said. "That man is dead, and it was not he who was outside last night."

Muriel's smile dropped. "It was him, wasn't it?"

She wished she'd picked up the fire poker as she stepped out onto the rough ground. She could guess who it was, but until she'd seen his face, there was that sliver of doubt that old Hobart Hurst had found a way back and had returned to torment them. "Step out and state your business," she spoke, sounding braver than she felt. There was no response, no movement, not a sound. The wind fought its way through the copse of trees. Clouds pulled across the sky towards the moon. "Are you too cowardly to show your face?"

"Don't mock me, you harlot."

Some of the low level terror dispersed. It was a stalker of flesh and blood. It was a relief to confirm that Hobart Hurst was not here, although she would not underestimate the problem of Horace Denver. He was an angry and irrational man, and the very fact he was loitering outside their home in the twilight hours was disconcerting. He could be dangerous, and seemed to be the bloodied minded sort who would hold a grudge till death.

"Horace Denver, you need to get back to your farm and mind your own. You stay away from harassing my family."

"You be damned to hell. You and your kind."

"How dramatic. It sounds as though Mr Denver indulges in far more gothic romances than I do."

"He's a fool."

"And a fool can be dangerous. He's a frustrated, repressed man." Eleanor finished her tea. "I don't know what he was doing skulking around the house. He's still angry that I passed a letter from his daughter to her sweetheart and now they are married. Best thing for her. It was a dreadful home, and I only spent one night there. What damage he must have inflicted on those children's minds as they grew up..."

"But this is a household of women," Emmerline exclaimed. "Has he no shame, terrorising you. He could come back?"

"He probably will."

"But you will never feel safe. What shall you do? Hire a man? Report him to the local constable?"

"For what?" Muriel muttered.

Eleanor raised her eyebrows and looked over at Emmerline. "We can take care of ourselves. A woman can shoot a pistol just as well as a man. Our best hope is that someone else annoys him and directs his fury elsewhere."

"You could always move."

"I will not be run out of my home."

Muriel looked down at the floor. Wasn't that why they'd left Whitby in the end?

"My main concern at the moment is your grandmother. This has upset her dreadfully. She has been forgetful of late, and this was an unnecessary stress for her."

"Might I go up and see her?" Emmerline asked.

Permission was granted, and she swept up the stairs, a princess on a rather more common staircase. When her grandmother saw her she began to sob. Emmerline hurried across to the bed where Maud was sat up, quilts upon her legs, her shoulders wrapped in shawls and a mop cap upon her white hair. The old lady smiled through her tears. "Oh Clara, my sweet, that I might see you again."

Emmerline grimaced before leaning forward. "It's Emmerline, grandmother. My mother..." she couldn't bring herself to say it. It had been so many years. It was distressing that she might be confused with her mother. Aunt Eleanor was correct in stating that the biggest worry ought to be the state of Maud's mind and constitution. She was unsettled and confused, yet trying to cover over. She smiled and nodded and blamed it on weak eyes, but that she could see now it was Emmerline. Of course it was. She neatly avoided the point that Clara was long since dead and couldn't possibly be here.

"Four children I had," Maud sighed. "And now only one lives. A parent ought not to live to see such things. And my girl Eleanor knows this sadness." She paused as if to drift away in her memories, then looked sharply at Emmerline. "And do you have children?"

"Not yet." Emmerline sighed. It was the same whenever her husband's family came to visit. That scrutiny, those well placed questions and a disappointed look as though the prize pig they'd brought back from market was not quite as good as they'd been promised. They'd already overlooked a disreputable family history, soothed away by a good fortune, but let it not be that the girl was barren as well. What was the point of such a woman if she would not furnish Moses Whitfield with a set of fine sons in his own image?

"There was a man outside last night," Maud whispered. "They don't believe me..."

"It was just a local farmer, from the moors."

"No." Her eyes widened. "I mean another one. My husband, your grandfather. He was here."

"Grandfather is dead."

"I know he is dead." Maud clutched her granddaughter's hands. Her own fingers were bony and angular, skin like paper. "I saw him die. He is dead..."

"I thought he disappeared?"

A sharp intake of breath. "I mustn't say. I forgot. I mustn't say. We must all follow the same story."

Emmerline felt her curiosity catch in the back of her throat. What family secrets were these? Did some of them really know what had happened? Her mother had always said he had been killed; only that she had been far from home at the time. Her belief had been a suspicion in other words. She leaned forward, trying not to show how keen she was for the old woman's memories. "What happened to grandfather?"

Maud caught her eye. "He disappeared. We don't know."

"But..."

Maud patted her hand. "I ought to rest now. It was very nice to see you again."

Emmerline was to stay for a few days. She wanted to spend time with her relations. She needed a break from the life of protocol and money, but also to avoid her own home and that man William John Scott who had taken it into his head that there was a spark between them. For her stay in Haworth she was rooming with Muriel and as the women were getting ready for bed, she had confessed to her cousin about her ulterior motive in coming to Haworth. Muriel had laughed the story off and told Emmerline she was far too pretty for her own good. It was not so much that she didn't believe her, as that she simply didn't comprehend. Emmerline didn't have to ask to know that Muriel had never had a sweetheart. She had far too many medical books in her room for her not to understand procreation, but she had no experience of emotions, of jealousy, of how far a man might go when he had decided he was going to take a woman. Emmerline didn't want to be pushed into that corner for she would defend herself. Then she would be to blame for the fall out. Here she was far too well known and there were far too many people about for her to get away with whatever she felt necessary.

"He doesn't still have that head with him?" Muriel asked drowsily, a joking smile fluttering across her face as she buried herself down into the blankets.

"Unfortunately so. He seems to mistake himself for a tribal man who sees holy significance in the object."

"It would be funny if you were right and it was a fake. A European head."

It was not amusing to hear the desperate tales of a trapped soul desperate for vindication he would never get. Emmerline sighed and stared up at the ceiling. She had always been brought up in high society, paying due deference to manners and behaviour acceptable to a lady of her station. She hadn't been wild and free as Eleanor's girls were. But she had known some state of independence when the family had stayed on the moors at Commondale. Life had never been quite as dull as when she had married. Sitting pretty at the dinner table decked out in jewels might be nice for one's vanity a couple of nights a year, but all the time?

Soon Muriel was snoring gently. Emmerline was as awake as a fresh morning prayer. She so wanted to fall into a slumber, certain here to be safe from roaming hands and chattering shrunken heads, yet her mind would not stop. Something was holding her back from slumber. Something or someone.

Heaving the blankets back at a corner, she swung her legs out onto the floor, wincing as the cold chill bit at her ankles. Slipping her feet into her boots, she moved quietly across the room and waited until she was in the hall before she lit a candle. She paused for a moment, listening to the burst of spark as the wick ignited and the intense glow leapt up, lighting the landing with a flickering half light. It was a curious home, a home certainly, but lacking in the family's history. Aunt Eleanor's husband had never even lived here. The family history and memories were back on the east coast. As she understood it, her grandmother Maud originated from Haworth, but even that connection was so long ago that many of her original contemporaries had passed away or moved on.

Here in West Yorkshire there was no connection back to the original Hurst roots. Hurst had been Maud's first married name, and maiden name of the aunts. Here there was no Hurst and yet something had risen. She walked down the stairs, careful to miss the creaking step, and reached the ground floor. She slipped down the passageway to the back door, following Maud's steps from last night. The key was hidden in the kitchen, but easily found, and Emmerline had the door unlocked and open in a moment. Last night there had been a breeze up and clouds shifting across the sky. Tonight it was unearthly still, not a cloud above, and a chill deeper than the grave seeping up out of the very earth.

For a moment she wondered what she was about, as she glanced across the open moorland in the distance, the copse of trees close by, then stepped out onto the frosty ground. The flame on the candle stood erect and motionless. Emmerline saw her breath frost out and disperse into the atmosphere.

A movement revealed that she was not alone. A man stepped out from the cover of the trees and approached. This was not the monster who farmed high on the moors. This was a short man, hunched over, and with a head that seemed a little too big for his body. Emmerline silently observed him as he walked closer, showing no sign of any emotion. She noted that his breath did not steam up in the air. He walked with a gnarled stick, he was old and his clothes were out of date. His shoes looked very well made.

"So you were here last night."

The old man stopped in front of her. He was a couple of inches shorter than Emmerline. As a pair they were a contradiction of age and youth, beauty and gnarled fury, of life and death. His eyes were very bright and alive as he regarded her.

"They thought there was only Denver."

"You are the only one. The only Hurst."

Emmerline smiled without joy. "I was never a Hurst. I was a Mowbray before I married."

"Only you have my blood."

Her eyes narrowed. She had picked up on rumours that her grandmother's children had been fathered by different men. It would account for the difference between all of the women, all of the families even. Was this why he was here, to see her? No, he would have come to her before now, and far more easily, had he wanted to. "You're a long way from your resting place."

"I have wandered this earth…"

"Why have you come here?"

"I have come for my wife."

"She's not dying."

"I can wait. I've been waiting a long time."

"You'll not torment her."

"I'll do what I like after…" his threats faltered as Emmerline held up a hand. He went silent, stared furiously at her for a moment, then broke into a crafty smile. "You most certainly are my Clara's daughter."

"Away with you, back to your pile of stones. You'll not bother these people as long as I live."

He nodded as if paying court and took a few steps back. "I will come back for her."

Emmerline's eyes narrowed. "Careful how you go. I don't think you are always best favoured amongst your own kind." She watched as he turned and strode out onto the moor, cutting a fast walking pace. As he turned the moon shone upon the back of his head and illuminated the sticky glistening hole. Not natural causes.

She was never quite sure what had happened to her grandfather or who knew the truth and who had been involved, but she had always felt it had been something close to home. Her mother had probably been correct in suspecting the worst of her own family.

Something had changed since Emmerline had seen her grandfather. It was not so much that Emmerline had changed, rather the interface between her and the world had become more perceptive. It would have been unsurprising if she'd found herself despising her family after all that she had learned. They knew about his disappearance/death. Her mother had been right to be suspicious, only that she hadn't realised the issue with secrets was that you were ignorant to the motives and circumstances.

Emmerline's change was as sudden and dramatic as if her eyes had opened for the first time. See one, then suddenly you see his kind everywhere. A week later, when she was travelling back to Wainstan Hall she saw two others of his ilk out of the carriage window. They were going about their business, working at the land in their native tracts, whilst she was merely passing through. One stopped at his labour, stood up and looked at her. For a moment their eyes locked in understanding. Then she was gone and he merged back in the background.

At moments it all felt too much. It had been bad enough hearing the voices of the dead. Now the world rushed in at her in such intricate detail. Information bombarded her at every moment, leaving her dizzy. Yet at Wainstan she was expected to be calm and dignified. She was the beautiful model to display jewels and dresses, the signs of a highly successful mill owner. She was to have polite conversation with the ladies at their dinner parties. Now that William John Scott and his shrivelled Dutch head had departed for their next adventure, there were no more 'entertainment' dinner parties, and the odd and the poor, as her husband regarded her relatives and the more eccentric of society, were no longer invited. The level of conversation dropped to monotonous society gossip, the latest fashions and who was secretly engaged to whom. Emmerline was caught in a strange tidal strip where she lingered static within utter boredom. She was locked in a room with closed windows shaking in their frames as the entirety of the universe tried to impose itself upon her. All the while she had to look serene, peaceful and at all times confident. It was around about that time she discovered that she was expecting her first child.

Muriel was another frustrated soul. She was desperate to be set lose on the world, yet was trapped in her role as spinster and woman. Never to think or learn or study, but supposedly to hang around waiting for a husband to appear. Increasingly irritated and unsettled, she announced to her mother that she was going to York for a few weeks to stay with friends. Eleanor trusted her enough not to query which friends she meant, and was probably still under the impression that Elizabeth was living in Scarborough, even though she had left that coastal town years ago. Elizabeth, the eldest daughter, and her mother had not spoken for years. Eleanor desperately missed her child but was still wounded by the disrespectful and underhand manner Elizabeth had manipulated people and events to her own tune. Eleanor was more saddened by the life choices she had made. On the other side of silence, Elizabeth missed her family, that much was clear by how she clung to the contact with her little sister, but was too proud. She was also far too busy keeping up the joyful, carefree facade that was the basic essential tool to keep her in business.

She pretended so much that she no longer knew when she was truly happy or sad.

Depending on whom you asked, Elizabeth included, she was a harlot, a prostitute, a whore, a kept woman, a courtesan, a failure, a disappointment and a brazen force of nature covering a distinct lack of confidence. After a brief employment as a lady's maid, she had become mistress to local nobility, who had set her up in a little home in Scarborough. That had lasted a few years before, depending on who was consulted, Elizabeth grew dull or the family money and generosity of her sponsor lessened, and they parted company. The final parting was well timed so that Elizabeth had her next gentleman in sights. He had gladly set her up in a fine little apartment in central York. The outrageous parties they held were talked about amongst circles of wealthy gentlemen. The ladies knew nothing apart from rumours they would never admit to having heard when in polite company.

According to the etiquette and decency of the time, Muriel and Elizabeth ought to have ceased all communication and acknowledgment. They walked in two different layers of society that were simply not fit to mix. Yet all they really had was one another. The family home in Whitby was essentially gone, their elder brother long dead and a home in Haworth that was more to do with Maud's heritage than anyone else's, likewise a place Elizabeth would never be able to attend. Eleanor was aware that the sisters exchanged letters but turned a blind eye to it. What she did not know was that Muriel still visited her elder sister. If there had been an inkling of suspicion whenever Muriel made a trip to York, she never let on, even to herself. And perhaps she still believed Elizabeth to be living in Scarborough in depravity. Muriel never dared ask her mother. Visits were timed between particular parties and extended stays by the gentleman sponsor. Muriel would travel to York with the post, and sneak into Elizabeth's property by the rear entrance. Society demanded its due and she could not be so bold as to hold an open acquaintance with the woman who had sold her virtue for money.

The journey had been a bumpy one in cramped conditions, jostled for many hours with strangers in the post carriage. Muriel knew she ought to be thankful that she had managed to get a seat inside, but it did grow tiresome being elbowed by some overweight gentleman who was having an animated discussion with a man opposite about the potential of railways. One day they would travel quickly and comfortably in steam driven, horseless carriages. A mechanised future promised great things. Never mind the looms and the weaving. That was just the beginning, mark his words.

Muriel was still wearing the mark of his words as the carriage finally arrived in York. Set free from the confines of stale air and conversation, she stood at the side of the street, stretching out the creases in her frame as the coachman slung down the cases. She fetched her little case – Muriel travelled light with only a few clothes and the essential books for reading – and decided to take a walk before she would try to sneak in to her sister's apartments unseen. She wandered aimlessly, lost in daydreams of a bright future and great scientific advancements and wished she could take part in all that excitement. She walked along by the river Ouse, and found herself down on North Street, by the dirty coal yards, warehouses and moorings for barges. So much noise, people hurried in business, transport, connection with the world. Muriel glanced about herself, caught up in the bustle of the working class and the poor. Some marched by, almost bumping into her on purpose and eyeing her smart clothes and the case she carried. She was in the wrong part of town. What was such a woman doing here?

Increasing her speed, she headed for the end of the road so that she might cross at the next bridge and return to the north side of the river and her sister's home. As she walked a gaggle of screaming, grubby children burst out of an alleyway, laughing and chattering in a jumbled mass of indistinguishable noise. From the calamity burst forth a little lad of three or four with a grave little face, clutching at a mewling kitten. He ran off from his comrades. So keen to escape, he did not look where he was going, but went straight into Muriel's backside. He stumbled back to the soundtrack of children's laughter.

"You know nothing, John Snow!" one of the lads shouted after him.

He and the kitten both looked up at Muriel. "Begging your pardon, missus," he excused himself before charging ahead to the bridge.

Muriel paused for a moment to watch the young lad disappear into the crowds. Her mind returned to her own problems. She needed to do something with her life. The apprenticeship at the jewellers was not for her. As interesting as it was to make mourning jewellery, she could not face it for the rest of her life. She would be thirty in a couple of years. She needed to find her way.

Regardless of what people might have said, Elizabeth MacCaskill was quite content that she had found her way in life. She lived in luxury and comfort with a cook and a maid to deal with those tiresome household chores and a gentleman to deal with the finances. She was no wife however, and did not to have to suffer under a weight of expectation marriage manacled women with. Where were the sons? What about her weekly church visits, her charitable acts? Social calls and engagements with polite society. How utterly dull. She did not have children, in-laws, social duties and expectations, and she didn't have to see him at his boring worst. Elizabeth enjoyed the pleasures of a man, and the pleasures of his generous purse, and was confident in her charms and abilities to know that when this ended in a few years, she would be moving up to an even greater gentleman. Although she was now thirty, she still had the glowing joyful look of a young buxom maid, her hair was still luxuriously dark and her eyes sparkled. She was always well rested and never weighted down with responsibility. There would be no children. Although she had taken precautions, these things had happened now and then over the years. Miscarriages had followed, and the doctor her current gentleman had paid, was now adamant she would be unable to have children. It was no bother to Elizabeth. A life without those screaming, snivelling little monsters was a life of freedom and enjoyment.

She laughed at nothing, as if to make that very point, and leant back into her seat, enjoying her glass of wine. Today she expected to see no one important, and had left her corsets off and her hair loose and unstyled. Her little sister, Muriel, had arrived this hour, sneaking into the building as if there was something to be ashamed of – no matter, at least she still kept up her connection with Elizabeth – and was now seated opposite, refusing wine and waiting for the tea that the maid would shortly bring.

"Do tell, how is mamma and our dear grandmother? Still enjoying suffering in the high winds of the moors?"

"They keep well and the house is proof against the winds."

Muriel regarded her sister in all her finery. She watched as she lifted the wine glass to her mouth. On the skin between finger and thumb junction there was the remains of an ulcer that had cleared leaving what would be a permanent indentation scar on the skin.

"Did you cut yourself?"

"What?" Elizabeth's brow creased for a moment, then she followed Muriel's line of sight to her hand. "Oh this," she waved it off as she set down her wineglass. "Just an ugly bump that came up on my hand. An ulcer or some such thing I suppose. It's all healed up now." She leaned forward and grinned wickedly, "You're not going to tell me I have the plague, are you? You still obsessing over those medical books, Muriel?"

She felt her face flush as if it were something to be embarrassed about. She was saved from more sisterly teasing as the maid arrived with the tea service. Elizabeth chattered away to the woman in French before sending her on her way. She was always careful to hire foreigners that spoke no English, finding it made life easier when they could not take part in local gossip. The cook usually had to be a native if only to deal with the tradesmen but the pay was always generous to ensure loyalty and discretion.

"And what of our dear little cousin?"

"Emmerline? She's expecting a child."

Elizabeth laughed, leaning forward gleefully. "So that old bore of a husband has finally proved his worth? Good thing she proved herself to be the prize pig they all thought she was."

"Emmerline's a very decent person. You shouldn't speak about her like that."

"Oh come, Muriel. Are you jealous of her? I see you're still without a ring upon your finger."

Muriel pursed her lips together and sat in silence for a few moments. She watched as her sister shuffled a little awkwardly and settled back in her chair. "This life makes you cruel and spiteful, Elizabeth."

"You mustn't mind my bawdy turn of phrase. It's the company I keep. It makes me direct. You know I only have wishes for your very best. How does it go, Muriel, seriously? Have you found peace with your jewellery profession? I can't say you look particularly contented."

"I don't think a craftswoman's life is for me," Muriel admitted.

"You are still pouring over those medical books." Elizabeth noted how Muriel still stared at her hand, probably desperate to diagnose. She pulled down her lace cuff to cover it. "You always did have to have a busy brain of learning. I remember you always staying with mamma in the office, bogged down in all those books. Learning, learning, learning. You even learnt those strange languages from the sailors who came to trade."

"Life is here to be explored."

"You spent too much time with that silly lad, what was his name? Went off with his father on those whaling ships as though he was the next Cook. What was his name? I am so forgetful these days."

"Scoresby," Muriel muttered.

"I'd always hoped you could enjoy the traditional route to a woman's supposed joy: a husband and children. That would have kept you busy. A doctor's wife would have been particularly fitting. I'm not saying it won't happen yet, but the years do march on." And Muriel still had a boyish figure, stubborn red hair and an off putting manner to amorous men, Elizabeth reflected. No man liked a woman who so obviously knew more about everything than he did.

"What rot from you. You hoped I would enjoy the traditional woman's life. Who are you to preach at me?"

"Are you suggesting I am beneath other women?"

"Society certainly does."

"You're being very evasive, Muriel. If that's how you feel, I'm surprised you come to see me at all."

"You are very vexing, Elizabeth, vexing and irrational."

"Irrational is avoiding life in the hopes of a woman being a doctor. Everyone knows only men can be doctors."

"Well, perhaps I'll just have to turn into a man, by some fancy manner of magic." Muriel abruptly rose from her chair. She could not look her sister in the eye. "I feel I have a headache coming on. I must lie down for an hour or two."

Lie down and read your precious books, Elizabeth thought sourly. She was unsettled for the rest of the evening. No visitors or parties, and a sulking sister in the spare room. She wandered aimlessly up and down her own boudoir, sorting her discarded dresses and petticoats, jewellery and hair pieces. A month or two ago a particularly drunken party had turned into something of an orgy and various items that did not belong to her had been left here. Ungrateful people cluttering up her apartments with their discarded clothing. She grabbed at shawls and breeches, shaking a fistful of shirt at her own reflection in the mirror. And with that shake, a germ of an idea sparked in her mind.

Overnight it would not go away, and indeed it was growing by the time she had risen the next morning. Muriel had left early in the morning for one of her rambles, so Elizabeth was left to amuse herself. She dressed early and decided to take a stroll about town – who cared if people stared. She was no common prostitute, but a mistress to English nobility and the shops would serve her and the general public would behave, even though respectable ladies would not associate with her, or even look her in the eye. Some could not help but dare a glance at her beautiful outfits, her tiny, corseted waist and her happy, radiant countenance, and she relished in the attention.

Through the centre of York she passed an older gentleman walking with a mannish woman dressed in black. The woman was unashamedly staring at Elizabeth, and even boldly met her eye and winked at her as the two passed. What unabashed frankness.

"Dr Belcombe," Elizabeth heard the woman speak as they walked on. "Do you know who that is?"

"Lord Nethercombe's mistress. Quite the scandal I assure you."

"Much the handsome woman. Does she have her own name?"

"Elizabeth MacCaskill. But that is one lady you shall not be making the acquaintance of during your stay with us this time."

"MacCaskill? How curious. Do you know I met a couple of MacCaskills over in Halifax? Quite the eccentric pair."

Dr Belcombe laughed out loud. "*You* found them eccentric?"

"Actually, I believe they were from Haworth, only I met them in Halifax."

Elizabeth paused and looked back the way she had come. The way that woman walked, one could almost believe she was a man. And she knew of Muriel and her mother? Poor Muriel, if the connection was to become better known.

At that moment Muriel was not concerned with her sister at all, but was crouching in a church yard some three miles north of York, in a little hamlet by the name of Huntington. When she was caught up in her thoughts, she could roam for miles, unable to stop or circle back, but inside having a basic need to move forward and away. She'd soon left the northern boundaries of York, passing by the Union Workhouse and following the track out of town, following to varying degrees a beck and passing through farmland with a scattering of cottages and farmhouses here and there. Coming down a slight bank, the road had swung around into a little hamlet clustered on either side of the road. She'd taken a turning in the village and crossed over the beck that had accompanied her thus far, to bring her to the village church.

"What are you doing?"

A rather adult question from a childish voice made her jump. There was a little lad with a kitten standing at the foot of the grave, staring rather sternly at her. Muriel squinted at him and realised she had seen him before, being chased by children in the centre of York. "Why, you're John Snow."

The lad's eyes snapped open in alarm. "How do you know me?"

"I saw you in town yesterday. Some children were chasing you."

"Aye, they like to do that. And what are you doing here? Do you have kin resting in this place?"

"No, I don't know anyone from these parts. I was taking a walk."

"I come from here. I was born in York, but me mother and me father were wed here five year ago. Then I came along."

Muriel couldn't help but smile. "And what a lucky pair they must be. Tell me, what does your father do, Master Snow."

"He works in the coal yard down by river. But he wants to be a farmer."

"Very wise. A profession better for the lungs I would suspect."

John nodded as if he knew this to be true.

"And what would you wish to be, Master Snow? A coalman or a farmer."

"I shall be an educated man."

She caught herself as she went to scoff. A poor working class family raising educated men. Why, it was almost ridiculous as women wishing to be doctors.

He nodded gravely at her and gently stroked the kitten's head. "They are saving money for me. They wish for me to have a better lot in life."

Why shouldn't he become an educated man? Why not? Muriel stood up. There had to be a way through every problem, one just had to reangle one's thinking to get there. "You have very considerate parents," she told him, looking to the sky and deciding it was time to head back to town. "Make sure you don't let them down."

"I won't." He nodded to Muriel before looking back down at the kitten and stroking it once more. "We're going to be educated men, aren't we kitty?"

That's it, Muriel thought. If the cat was to be an educated man, why shouldn't she?

They only really got down to business when Elizabeth finally accepted that her sister did indeed speak fluent French. In the beginning Elizabeth insisted on translating word-for-word everything that the maid said. Muriel was furious, listening and understanding the rapid chattering between Elizabeth and her maid, then forced to listen to Elizabeth's haughty translations. Whilst Elizabeth impressed no one switching between languages, the maid grew sulky thinking she was not being taken seriously.

Muriel walked down the length of the room, turned and regarded her sister and the ladies maid. Elizabeth stared approvingly at her legs, but Nolwenn shook her head. "You do not have it," she declared in rapid French as Muriel met her eye uncertainly. "Women are not certain of their place outside the home. A man knows it. He does not question."

Her confidence had been as high as the heavens when she had returned from her walk. She had told Elizabeth that she was going to university. She would study to become a doctor. She had the intelligence and interest and she was going to show the world just what a woman could achieve. Elizabeth, reclining like a wilted flower in her favourite chair, had fluttered her fan in her face and shook her head in amusement, as if pacifying a child that had no grasp on reality.

"No, no, no."

"You doubt my ability?"

"I am quite sure you have the ability and the intelligence. But the world will not accept a woman wishing to study medicine. You can fight the world on behalf of womankind and you will achieve nothing. If you wish to achieve anything, you must achieve it for you. And you must twist the rules to suit your purpose."

"What are you suggesting? I marry a doctor?" Muriel said sourly.

"No. I say you become the doctor." Elizabeth stood up and shook out a pair of trousers. "Some fool who was here the other week abandoned his clothes. I say if someone doesn't re claim their possessions after three days then they are mine. And as my property I do pass them to you."

Muriel took the trousers and stared at the fabric, a little horrified. "You wish me to wear these?"

"And the rest. Muriel, you have a slight frame and a boyish countenance. We shall use it to our advantage."

"Lie?"

"Play a role. We all play roles to get what we want, to get us through lives. You see confident people in professions, and you assume that what they show you is what they are. You have no idea what is under the surface. Why, some of the people who call themselves doctors in these parts have not even studied at an institution. Believe me, people tell me all kinds of things at my parties, for they think I am outside of good society and therefore it does not matter. Consider it, Muriel. Only men may study medicine at Edinburgh. So we shall send them a man."

And so Elizabeth and Nolwenn dressed her up in shirt, trousers, waistcoat and jacket. Elizabeth even found an old broken pocket watch abandoned one night by her sponsor and amour. In the disguise they set her to pace the room. Muriel had to admit that the clothes were a good fit; they must have originally belonged to a slight and of average height man. But it was strange to walk in her stocking feet and have nothing about her legs. She felt naked waist down, yet her legs were clothed as if in sleeves for the lower body.

"You're walking as if you're wearing a skirt," Elizabeth realised. "You need to stride more."

"Confidence!" Nolwenn commanded, enjoying this afternoon's task.

Muriel looked like a frightened mouse. "Everyone will know."

"Only if you let them see. If you walk in to the room and tell them you are a man, what reason would they have to think otherwise?"

"We need to do something about her hair," Nolwenn spoke to Elizabeth. "We must cut it off."

"Yes."

"No." Muriel stopped abruptly. "Absolutely not."

"There, your body stance is more like it."

"Why can we not cut your hair?"

"I can't be a man here in Yorkshire. I can't go home to Mamma and tell her I am a man."

"That is something to be considered. I suppose you will need to be able to slip back into your natural way sometimes. But it would be too risky to travel with women's things. I know, you shall leave your dresses here, then when you need to switch, you can come to my apartments first, arrive as one person and depart as the other."

Muriel jumped as Nolwenn's hand was suddenly on the back of her neck. She hadn't noticed the maid move.

"We cut it here close. Then I can keep the hair, fashion it as a hair piece as it is now. It can be pinned to the head when you are a woman. No one need know that you cut your hair."

"And these clothes are such a sharp fit," Elizabeth said as she circled her sister closely. She tugged at the jacket by the arms. "Take it in a little at the shoulders. Really, we could just send these clothes to a tailor and ask him to run up a couple more of the same size."

"A neckerchief to hide her slender throat."

"Oh yes, my darling has an old cravat he never uses. It's been left here for months. You can have that. And then we shall invite my doctor over and quiz him on how we get you into Edinburgh."

"I doubt a medical man would help us with this."

"Of course he will. He's not going to meet Muriel. He'll meet your masculine self. We'll need a name and a history to give him. What should we call you? I know, Oscar Hammond."

Nolwenn pursed her lips. "She looks a bit odd for an English man."

"We'll say he's a foreigner. People will accept any strangeness if they know a man is not an Englishman."

Nolwenn snorted. The arrogance of the English never ceased to irritate her, even after all this time in the country. She had picked up enough of the language to understand but never felt inclined to speak to people in their local tongue. She could not say how many times she had heard a discussion start with: 'An Englishman would not...' In her experience nationality meant nothing. All men had a baseness to them and given the right set of circumstances were capable of anything, English or not.

"What about a nice French name, Nolwenn?"

The maid pouted at the doctor-to-be. "Have you ever been to France?"

"No."

"Too many people here have. I think they will find holes in your history. Your French is very good of course, not like a native but I could train you, but I think people will trip you up on the facts. You need to be from somewhere obscure."

"Somewhere no one knows anything about the country."

"What about Armenia?"

"I still need to know enough to be convincing. I am going to a great seat of learning; I will come across someone who will test me. I don't speak a word of Armenian."

"A lot of the aristocracy don't speak the language of their land. They are brought up on French and German."

"I am not an aristocrat."

"What about that funny little state in Russia the sailors were always coming from? You used to speak with them as a child in Mamma's office."

"Estonia. I do remember it well."

"Well, there we go. You read up on the state, brush up on your Estonian, and we'll make a doctor of you yet."

"I learnt it from sailors. My accent is probably very rough."

"You just said you aren't an aristocrat."

Elizabeth clapped her hands together, her face glowing with excitement. "Goodness, this is fun. Nolwenn, get my writing desk. I'm going to write a note to my doctor immediately, invite him for tea and a consultation tomorrow. Tell him I'm going to introduce him to an earnest young man I've made an acquaintance with. What were those old sailors called?"

"I remember one called Kaarel."

"Excellent."

"Perhaps the name should start with M," Nolwenn suggested. "You will react better when someone shouts to you."

Muriel flicked back through her memories of the old sea dogs and captains that had come bartering and trading at the offices in Whitby. Had anyone been called something starting with M? A face loomed up in her mind. That of a Captain Must. "Must," she said decidedly, looking up at Nolwenn without question, but a very definite introduction. "My name is Kaarel Must."

Kaarel Must began his medical studies at the University of Edinburgh in the autumn of 1817. He was the only Estonian student, but not the only foreigner, and whilst a little different, he paid his way and did not stand out as a trailblazer. He revelled in his secret, but walked a bold and confident walk, as trained by the French maid, Nolwenn. Now at his destination he got down to the serious business of absorbing as much knowledge as was offered.

Elizabeth MacCaskill's doctor had been taken by the odd young man, intensely curious as to his connection with the Yorkshire courtesan. By the end of their meeting he had been laughing as if after an agreeable evening of intoxication at the inn and said he would write Must a letter of recommendation. The money was available to cover the fees, and he had been accepted into the historical seat of learning. A lot about it surprised him, not least the fact that there was no compulsory curriculum or point at which the university would deem a man qualified. There were fewer men present than Kaarel had presumed. Students were plenty, but most of the students were only in their mid teens: a mixture of pompous little youths continuing with Pappa's trade; grave, serious young masters who would go far in the history of medical development; and those who would never amount to more than negligent fools who made money out of poor people's miseries and gave exacting example to the phrase 'a little knowledge is a dangerous thing.' The doctor at York had recommended a couple of years at Edinburgh to bolster the book learning Kaarel had obviously applied himself to, and then to get an apprenticeship with a doctor, surgeon or apothecary to gain the practical life experience that would set him up to go confidently in practice himself. Whichever branch he chose to follow.

Kaarel secured lodgings a five minute walk from the Old College where the medical school was housed, providing lectures to earnest students. From there it was a jump across South Bridge Street to head down Infirmary Street where the Infirmary providing practical experience was available. It was a densely built up city of hard grey Scottish rock born of the earth's beginning. There was a stubborn solidity about the rock that would withstand anything the atmosphere may throw at it. This was a world above the places Kaarel had been before: Halifax, Haworth, Whitby and York: which felt like provincial towns in comparison. Even York, with its status of capital of the north felt small and humble.

In the city of Edinburgh masses of people were everywhere. It was exhilarating to hear the language of the father MacCaskill, remembered from a childhood. Here were his people. The city hummed with businesses, schools, enterprises and cramped homes everywhere one looked. Why, even in the short perimeter of Kaarel's study-intensive world there were breweries and riding schools, graveyards and churches, all set below the looming might of the castle on Castle Hill to the west and Salisbury

Crags and Arthur's Seat – a great mountainous wilderness – to the east.

There were other medical students lodging at Must's quarters, most of them at least a decade younger than the Estonian. There was a Scot from Applecross who was a couple of years older than Must. Life wasn't silver spoons for everyone and it had taken some time to save the money necessary for an education. He had worked at apothecaries and highland surgeries for paid experience before he was able to get himself to Edinburgh. Their ages marked that the road had been neither easy nor straightforward and it was an achievement that they had reached the university. That and the fact that their maturity gave them more to relate over than the boys still growing into their adult bodies meant they were a little different to many of the students. Perhaps it was simply destined that Kaarel Must and Erskine MacKenzie would become fast friends. Erskine joked that between the two of them, they already had the knowledge to be a fully qualified and experienced doctor, for he had the years of experience assisting experienced professionals in the highlands and on the Isle of Skye, whilst Kaarel had an astounding mental library of all that could be memorised from the medical books in print. There was not a Latin term that Kaarel did not know, nor an ailment or disease he had not come across on the pages of textbooks. Erskine wanted to increase his book learning and Kaarel wished to gain the practical experience, each set on furthering their careers. They were also united in their bilingualism. Although the Gaelic was being repressed throughout Scotland, Erskine admitted one quiet evening that he spoke it fluently – it was not something for Edinburgh – whilst Kaarel, from the Russian Empire and state of Estonia, spoke his mother tongue of Estonian. As well as the French and the German that many scholars had.

Erskine MacKenzie was a relaxed, softly spoken dark-haired Scot who carried an unprepossessing confidence in what he did. He had an easy, reassuring way with the patients in the Infirmary and could settle a panic or help calm a patient who was falling into death regardless of their reluctance to accept. It was in part life experience, of watching old hands at work, but also an innate quality he was born with, quite simply something that could not be taught. One either could or one couldn't. He put down Kaarel's moments of awkwardness to a Baltic trait and language and cultural issues. Even so, he would joke sometimes when they had been enjoying a little too much wine that Kaarel could have been a proper Scot if he wished, with hair as red as that. He had never imagined that the Slavs had such complexions and hair. No, Kaarel had responded, people either think we are all blonde and sun deprived, or dark haired and continental, heavy browed and inclined to too much introspection. Erskine's hair would not have been out of place on the streets of Tallinn. Erskine had laughed heartily and suggested in jest they had been swapped at birth under some mystic reasoning, only to be brought back together as they came to study their life's work.

Kaarel enjoyed the theoretical lectures, the time spent in the Infirmary visiting patients, and surprised both himself and others by immediately taking to anatomy and dissection without such much as a shudder. He showed a steady and accurate hand with the knife, and whilst some students found they needed extra tuition in this area, some even going to Robert Knox's private lectures, Kaarel showed a natural flair. Fast, precise and without hesitation, there were mutterings that this would be the next great surgeon. Kaarel wondered this as well, until he attended his first surgery lecture, to sit and observe an operation on a woman who needed to have a tumour removed from a breast.

It was not the mess, the interior gore or the butchery of the matter that caused distress. In fact, had the woman been a rotting corpse, Kaarel could have stepped down the rows of observation benches to the bull ring in the centre where the work was conducted, and performed the procedure himself. But this was not a corpse in a dissection class. Regardless of how much the woman's doctor had advised her this was necessary, no matter how sure she was, the terror hummed in her eyes as she was brought in to the operating theatre and strapped down. There were two assistants, large, muscular Scottish men in thick aprons who loitered to one side. To begin with their presence seemed pointless as if they had arrived at the wrong show. They came in to their own when the operation started and the woman began to scream. She was sober and alert and could feel the cut of the knife and the parting of skin and flesh. The warm flow of blood alerted her panic and she tried to lurch from the table, despite the straps. The assistants held her down. The intensity of the screams filled the auditorium and the students were silent. Even the professor at work was visibly struggling to explain what he was doing in a calm and clinical manner.

Something dropped out of Kaarel's stomach. Empathy flooded his system as though someone had stabbed his own breast with a dull knife. He closed his eyes, sensing a cold sweat breaking out across his face. He was feeling quite feint. His rate of breathing rose and panic consumed him with a sudden need to flee the room. He almost tripped over his own feet to get out of the row and up the staircase. No one heard his movement for the screaming of agony was too loud. It followed him out of the room and down the corridor. Even as the doors burst open to eject him from the building, the intense human suffering followed him like a nauseating stench. The air outside was cold but he was burning up, his collar too tight at his throat. He ran a short distance, started up some stone steps that led to the next road, on a higher level to Infirmary Street, then swung around, hitting the palms of his hands against the wall as vomit spewed up out of his mouth, splattering to the ground and smearing his shoes. He pressed his forehead to the wall and closed his eyes. No more.

"Goodness man, you surprise me," a voice spoke, growing louder as it approached. "You've never so much as hesitated in a dissection, even the very first."

A warm hand rested on Kaarel's back.

"My dear friend, are you feeling quite well?"

Kaarel took a handkerchief from his pocket and wiped his mouth. He was shocked by how much his hand was shaking. "It was not the blood."

Erskine nodded sagely. "This is the thing that book learning cannot prepare you for."

"I've seen people suffering in the infirmary. I've seen people die."

"Aye, but the agony of surgery."

Kaarel straightened up. "It is butchery. Surely there is something that can be given to dull the senses..."

Erskine shook his head. "There's not much. A wee nip for courage perhaps, whisky, you know. But the pain is a good thing. It encourages the system to self heal. If they did not feel it, they might just slip away. I've seen it before, with gangrene, which is a little different but..."

"Good God, man, it's torture in there. We are a civilised society."

"Disease is no respecter of civilisation." He patted Kaarel's arm. "A lot of people react like this the first time. Nothing to be ashamed of. You think of those laddies that had to leave the room when they brought the first body for us to study..."

"I say it again," Kaarel interrupted, his speech a little more vigorous. He straightened himself, pushing back from his friend. "It is not the gore; it is the lack of humanity shown to that woman. I have not come to be a medieval torturer. Perhaps I have come to the wrong profession. I should try law perhaps..."

Erskine laughed out loud. "There are plenty who would suggest the law is the very birthplace of torture."

"I say again, I cannot do it. I may have to leave Edinburgh."

"You're overreacting, man," Erskine called after him as Kaarel started up the steps. "It was only your first, and even then, so what if you're not meant to be a surgeon. There's plenty of avenues to follow." He took a couple of steps forward as Kaarel reached the next street. "You've too much natural talent for this to throw it all away."

Kaarel shook his head miserably. "I cannot do this." He hurried down the street, and out of Erskine's sight, feeling an utter fool. Reading books was no replacement for real life experience. Who had he been to think a woman could cope with all this? They had their reasons for keeping women out of universities and now he knew why.

Lydia was five months old when Muriel first met her. Emmerline, who was almost recovered in energies from the birth, regarded her cousin with some concern when she came to visit. She had lost weight and colour, but aside from the physical changes, it was the great burden of worry she carried that haunted her. Muriel did not attempt to hide any of the distress either, even her hair was fixed up in an odd style which was not becoming to her.

"Where have you been this past year? Your letters have been quite vague and Aunt Eleanor has been worried. Seeing you has not erased any concerns I had."

"Oh, this and that," Muriel waved off the questions, wan and distracted, and gazed off down the length of the garden to mark that the subject was closed. The trees in the distance were just starting to change, tinges of autumn hues appearing in their leaves.

"That hardly answers the question at all. Are you in some trouble?"

Muriel looked sharply at Emmerline. Perhaps not, she thought, certainly not the usual types of trouble judging by the expression on her cousin's face.

"I just made a mistake with a choice of occupation. Just like the mourning jewellery, it was not for me."

"And now you find yourself drifting without aim." Emmerline concluded. "Oh, you should come here more often and keep me company. Or come on a trip with us. My husband wishes to go to Manchester next year to see new machinery and business ventures and wants the family with him. I don't know why, but you should come with me."

"Manchester?" Muriel did not sound impressed. "It's a rather industrial place. What is there to do?"

"Oh, I don't know. I am assured we will be staying in a very exclusive area. And then perhaps we will travel onwards to the countryside. Buxton perhaps. It will be very pleasant."

Spending weeks anywhere near Emmerline's husband did not appeal to Muriel. "Next year is a long time away," she finally said.

"It will soon be here, won't it?" Emmerline looked down at the little baby who was perched upon her mother's lap. Bright little alert eyes pierced Muriel without apology.

"And how does motherhood suit you? Does it keep you very busy?"

"Not as busy as I would like. He insists there is a hired staff for Lydia, for it wouldn't look right for a wife of his to be feeding and up at night. So she has her own nurse and nursery attendant and I am permitted to play with her now and then."

"Different to some mothers I would guess. Those that have to do all the care and run the home."

"Oh, but those women are bred for it."

Muriel cocked an eyebrow. "Those women."

"Well, they are different, the lower classes."

Muriel snorted at such nonsense. "You've been listening to your husband too much. There's nothing between you and those women apart from chance of birth."

"Yes, well..."

"Ma'am."

The bickering was interrupted by the arrival of the nursery attendant. A neat woman, immaculately dressed and very sure on what a child should and should not do. "It is time for Miss Lydia's nap. Might I take her in?"

"It is? Why, yes, of course." Emmerline passed the child across. The two cousins sat on the picnic cloth in silence for some minutes, Emmerline growing increasingly agitated. "I should know when her naps are. Why don't I?"

"Because you don't look after her. You are not the one who decides."

"I am her mother."

Muriel shrugged absently and raised her face to the sun. "You live in a very strange world. I don't think I'd care for it."

Emmerline was about to laugh at such nonsense, she was at the peak of modern society and of course everyone would aspire to her place. But on reflection there were plenty of things about her existence that irritated her. "Will you not take a parasol?" she changed the subject, spinning hers to make a point. "You'll go brown like a labourer sitting in direct sun like that."

"I can't say I'd care. Besides, it feels good." She opened her eyes and looked at Emmerline. She had regained much of her health since the birth but looked a little lost in her mind and place in the world. "How was it?"

"What?"

"The birth."

"Oh, better now it's just a memory."

"You may have to do it again."

"They say it gets easier after the first. You know, I really shouldn't say anything to you about it, what with... well, you being a spinster."

"I'm not allowed to know?"

"No, but what if you should ever get married? What if you fell with child? You'd be worried."

I've seen women giving birth, Muriel thought. I've sat beside people who died in agony. I've been up to my wrists in blood and gore. I know more than you ever will. But no one talks about feeling and experience with the doctor in that way.

"Well, I can't say it was pleasant at the time."

Muriel laughed. "It was unpleasant? Oh Emmerline, what strong language you use."

Emmerline burst out laughing. "Oh, I know you and your strange reading habits. You probably know more about it all than I do. You know what pain is like. As soon as it's a memory you convince yourself it wasn't all that bad and you'd be able to cope with it again if you needed to. But at the time it's as if you're being tortured in hell. The pain... all I could do was scream."

"Do they not give you anything for it?" Muriel thought of the women in the operating auditorium. Of course they didn't give anything for childbirth. They said the pain was an important part of the process, and important for the child to be born. A few of the old-testament leaning also felt that it came part and parcel of Eve's sin and suffering to be borne by all woman kind. Muriel had heard a lot of scorn for women whilst she had been in Edinburgh.

"No, the doctor was quite adamant. But I think..." Emmerline stopped, looking guilty as though she was about to tell something terrible. "I think if I should do it again, I would take something. There are some plants that you can use to ease the pain."

"You're talking about those old midwives. Their herbal remedies."

"Much can be done with plants. I found some old diaries of my mother's."

"There's still things of Aunt Clara's left?" Muriel sounded shocked. Emmerline's mother was in a similar grouping as Elizabeth: relatives not spoken of. Not that Clara had ever sold her sex; she had been a highly respectable married lady. But she had been executed for murder, and Eleanor muttered darkly about Clara sometimes, that she had been able to manipulate situations and people. She had been an underestimated and dangerous woman.

"Not much, and I keep it hidden. I'm sure he would burn it if he knew," she referred to her husband. "But she mentioned some things she prepared when I was born, to help with the pain. I only took note when I was re reading some passages a few days ago. Lydia is an utter joy and anything was worth it for her, but to feel like that again, as though the very flesh of me was to be wrenched up into my own body..."

Muriel squeezed her wrist. "It's over and done with now."

"There'll be more. He's desperate to have a son."

"It'll be quicker next time. And think, the human race has been having babies for thousands of years."

"And back in pagan times I'm sure they let the women use their plant knowledge to its full extent. Next time I shall make sure it will be easier."

Next time, Muriel noted. Her cousin was brave. Despite the pain and terror, she was prepared to do it again. And it was a pain personally experienced. Muriel was not even brave enough to face the suffering of another human in the operating theatre. She was not brave enough to return to Edinburgh and continue her studies, knowing that everyone knew that she had run away. For they knew, the moment the screaming started, she would be gone again.

And so Muriel listlessly drifted through the weeks and months. Only her sister, Elizabeth, had any real idea of what might have happened, especially after discussion with her own doctor. She learned that some young men found the realities of medicine too much. But perhaps the young man could be persuaded down a less brutal avenue? There was always pharmacology, or perhaps anatomy. The dead did not feel pain. Elizabeth wrote several times with good advice, but it was as much as Muriel could manage some days to open a letter, let alone reply. She fell into a pit of remorse and regret, lost weight off an already thin frame and looked wan and corpse-like.

Life is short, Eleanor thought as she stood at the back of the graveyard, trying to keep her mind on the current event. Even with this in front of her, her thoughts returned to Muriel. She was not exactly sure where Muriel had gone all those months. She had been told a vague story about an assistants job at a chemist somewhere north, but Muriel would not be drawn on the details, nor explain why it had ended and why she had come home. Eleanor could understand if Muriel's heart wasn't in it, for many projects had started and ended within six months, simply not offering the mental challenge Muriel needed. But she had never been this withdrawn when another possibility failed. She had still been busy with her books and lectures, thinking and pondering, out walking and keeping busy. Now she haunted her room mostly and gazed miserably out of the window. For a time Eleanor had worried that Muriel had been love sick, a man had been involved somehow and perhaps she was in trouble and didn't know how to ask for help. But the monthly bloody rags continued to appear and Muriel grew thinner. If it was a love issue, it was an unrequited love which was the worst to suffer from.

Anne Thwaite, the housekeeper, suddenly gripped Eleanor's forearm tightly. "Here they come."

The two women shifted in position to gaze down towards the top of the hill where the street came up to the church. A great mass of locals gathered in subdued limbo, awaiting for the main body of mourners: the relatives, the professionals and the diligent churchgoers. Spring was in full force, the sun shone and the day felt glorious, yet it was a sad day for the top of the hill, for Mr Charnock, priest to this locality had passed away just a few days gone. Now in his wooden box, he was carried by sweating men up the hill towards his final resting place. The site of his work would be the situation of his eternal rest. Eleanor had not been a regular face at church, yet she had felt compelled to attend the funeral.

Anne's eyes were darting across the sea of faces, taking it all in. "There must be a hundred people here," she whispered. "He was well respected, was Mr Charnock. Many folk want to pay their respects. Any other funeral and I might have gone to the house for the start of the procession, but what with his popularity I thought I'd start up here with you. Will you be attending the arvill afterwards?"

Eleanor shook her head. She had not been a church goer and had not been that close to the man. There would be too many more worthy people wishing to attend the funeral meal afterwards. Her eyes settled on the coffin as it came through the gate. This is what it all amounts to, she thought miserably. Rotting bones. Mr Charnock was of the same vintage as she. Who knew how many days she had left on this earth. Perhaps it would be a long time, her own mother still lived, although her mind crumbled. But of the four Hurst children born to Maud, only Eleanor still lived. Even two of Eleanor's own children were long dead. Her dear husband was dead these last ten years. Life was cruel and illogical; she could not make sense of the twisted patterns it wove, or the reasons why. What exactly was the point of all this meant to be? Was living even the lucky option, to be left increasingly alone, missing those who had gone and wishing them back with no hope.

Anne's grip tightened slightly as she spotted someone of interest. "There's Mr Heap," she hissed, pointing out a man towards the head of the funeral procession, obviously someone of importance. "Vicar of Bradford."

"Oh," Eleanor sighed. She had little interest in the Yorkshire hierarchies of clergymen.

"Given himself delusions of grandeur he has. Mr Charnock not in his grave, and Mr Heap is already meddling. Thinks he's in charge of us here in Haworth, but he's not."

Eleanor glanced over at the housekeeper, a little surprised by the determined rebellious note in her voice. "What do you mean meddling?"

"Rumour has it he's going to offer the position to an Irishman."

"You don't like the Irish?"

Anne's eyes widened in despair that her employer wasn't following what ought to be an obvious affront to every resident of Haworth. "It's not up to him to go offering the position," she whispered, wanting to show respect as the procession started to take up position for the start of the ceremony, but at the same time desperate to impart her gossip. "He's just going about it as if the opinion of the trustees doesn't matter."

"The trustees?"

"Of the church." Anne nodded at the building to which they all clustered. "Mrs MacCaskill, I know you are a newcomer to these parts, but you've been here long enough to know what's what."

"Yes, yes, of course." Eleanor patted Anne's hand. "My mind is just distracted today."

Distracted certainly, but had Eleanor been in peak mental condition, she would not have cared one jot for who was to take up the curacy of St Michaels, and even less about the grief between Bradford and Haworth, and who wasn't showing due deference or respect to who. All these vicars and curates and trustees and ancient bylaws and traditions holding up fine church buildings that poor and suffering folk attended when they'd be better resting on a Sunday and for what? For a belief that preached kindness but worried more about tradition, rules, judging people's behaviour and condemning those with ill fortune in life.

Despite her lack of interest, over the following weeks Anne kept her up to date with all the scandalous goings on. The Irishman, as it turned out was a very decent fellow that they all heartily approved of, for he turned down the curacy when he learned of all the controversy that surrounded the position. He must be a good man if he was not coming. Good or wise, Eleanor mused. No matter, folk seemed very pleased with themselves that they had no vicar and had scared off one potential man for the position, who sounded very fitting. And regardless of the trouble caused by Haworth seeing off his first choice, Mr Heap continued in his endeavours of controlling everything without consultation, and gave the curacy to Mr Redhead, feeling that as the man had covered many a service during Mr Charnock's illness, he would be naturally accepted by the locals.

"It's a disgrace!" Anne shrieked as she stomped about the corridors in her clogs. She had come to the house early to see about Maud's breakfast, before she was to attend Mr Redhead's first service.

"Then you are going to church?"

"Of course."

"But you don't approve of Mr Redhead?"

"We're all going to show him. Word's been round. We're all going in our clogs."

Eleanor's brow wrinkled. She did not follow the logic, if there indeed was any. "That will show him," she said vaguely, as Anne headed off to church. She was not quite sure what Anne Thwaite's clogs would show Mr Redhead, or indeed what anyone's footwear would do.

Muriel, curled up in an armchair by the fire, rubbed her bleary eyes. "Just as long as I don't have to listen to her stomping about in those wooden things anymore. My head feels dreadful."

"You'd feel better if you ate properly."

"I'm not a child," Muriel muttered.

Later in the day Anne regaled them with the great clog success of that Sunday. The church had been packed for Mr Redhead's service, the pews were full and there were even folk standing in the aisles. Mr Redhead had looked confident, certain he had automatically won over the entire locality. What a fool! They let him prattle on for some time, before they stood up as one united team, and left the church. Oh, Mrs MacCaskill, you should have heard the din all those clogs made. She had laughed gleefully at this. There was none but Mr Redhead and his clerk to see the service to the end.

Mr Redhead was either stubborn or determined to win them over, for the mass walk out did not perturb him. He was back the following week for another service. He had probably hoped that having made their point, people would settle back into their place in society and show deference to the church. Give up all that nonsense and remember they were here to honour God.

Eleanor MacCaskill was just breathing relief as she completed the last steep pull up the hill when the donkey clattered out of the church and onto the street, braying furiously and desperately trying to shake the drunk from its back. From the church there was the sound of laughter where there ought to be that of angelic singing or the peal of bells. The parishioners began to pour out of the building, some holding hats which they waved at the drunk, now on the ground, to say he'd lost his headwear. He'd certainly lost his donkey, for the beast had fled up the street and away to the moors.

More trouble for Mr Redhead, Eleanor thought, silly man. He ought to take the hint that he was not wanted here and find a quiet little parish to serve. But Mr Redhead would not be budged and was back in the pulpit the following Sunday. This time a drunken chimney sweep was sent up to him, the poor inebriated sot trying to clamber into the very pulpit with the preacher, egged on by eager locals. The mood swiftly darkened when it looked as though even this affront would not stop the unwanted man. Mr Redhead tried to fight off the chimney sweep, before giving up. He tried to get himself out of the pulpit. The churchgoers were growing angry, and had tried to grab at the man. He was physically slung out of the church and into a heap of soot left earlier. The priest, perhaps now finally understanding how unwanted he was, managed to break free from the grasping hands and fled out of the churchyard. He dashed to the Black Bull, where the landlord swiftly barred the doors. People in the crowd were threatening to stone Mr Redhead, and for a morning the mood was dark. Eleanor missed that spectacle but heard about it later and was left thinking on the rioting in Whitby she'd seen (and if she was honest, partially instigated) in fury at the pressgangs. Which was a worthy cause, she felt, in comparison to a complaint of Bradford choosing Haworth's priest, but then, an Englishman's home was his castle and people did take exception to outsiders deciding for them.

Mr Redhead did not return for a fourth Sunday, much to Anne Thwaite's and many other's delight. The church was then in something of a limbo, but after discussion and inclusion of the trustees, it was agreed to return back to the beginning and accept the original choice, as he had shown such decency in turning down the position when he had heard that Haworth did not want him. The Irishman was currently at Thornton, but would pack up his family and be in the new curacy for the New Year.

Manchester loomed out of steam and smoke, a surreal industrial landscape appearing layer by layer. It was futuristic, honouring the might of technology and forward-looking whereas everywhere she had been before was tied to what had been. They said there were eighty steam-powered spinning mills, each with its own towering brick built chimney belching forth smoke. The houses were stained black and in town one never enjoyed an utterly clear day with a full blast of sunshine. The bass of heavy pistons pumping keeping the mass production going was the life beat of the city. This was the global capital of cotton, dressing the world in high quality fabric. Nothing was as they had seen before, even the very water looked wrong. In the rivers and canals the water was unnatural from the dyes spilling out into the waterways.

Edinburgh was a big city, but that was an ancient place of learning, wisdom, hill and crooked alleyways. A city built on levels, a compacted massing of history. Here was efficiency. Here lived profit and high yield, the latest in factory machinery and engineering. Here was where the money was being made. Muriel's brain was overwhelmed on first acquaintance and her maladies forgotten.

How on earth did it all work? Her mind demanded.

The winter in Haworth had not been good. Muriel had done little, her books ignored and her walks and visits neglected; she sank deeper and deeper into listless silence. Her mother had tried all kinds of methods to get through to her, but nothing worked and she would not confide in anyone. Her sister, Elizabeth, had heard somehow that Muriel was no longer in Edinburgh, but feeling sorry for herself back at home. She'd sent some books with suggestions of what Muriel ought to do to get out of the doldrums. *Fanny Hill*, Muriel had wondered, before her eyebrows had shot up on sight of the illustrations and descriptions. She'd dealt with enough patients and illnesses and read far too many anatomical books for any angle of the human body to shock her. But this brought something new to her reading, and what people chose to do with their bodies made her feel a little feint. She'd burnt the books on her bedroom fire, terrified that her mother might come across such illicit material and ask what she was doing with it, or more importantly, how she had come across it. Not that Muriel had to tell her anything just because she asked. She had become very adept at keeping secrets.

Emmerline had visited with her little girl Lydia, and had little success, but she and Eleanor were agreed that something needed to be done. They eventually got Muriel out to Wainstan Hall in the summer, and from there she joined the family on their trip to Manchester, followed hopefully by Derbyshire afterwards. Whilst Manchester was fascinating, one did not go there for the air. They were to stay in a fine townhouse in Ancoats whilst Moses Whitfield, Emmerline's husband, took his fill of visiting factories, examining new machinery and meeting with trading partners and contacts. Pompous rich men strutting about, Muriel thought as she caught sight of them one morning in the smoking room, each rather full of his own importance. There were mutterings of Luddites and thank God that was all over now, such unruly types hung. But there were still agitators, you know. Man alive, had you heard what was happening in France? There were still lazy worthless layabouts who thought rather than working for their living, they had the damned right to fight an honest factory owner for more money. More than money, didn't you know some of them wanted the vote? That got plenty of laughs. One couldn't give the vote to the common man, why, he did not have the intelligence to know what to do with such a thing, he would bring the country to ruin. Let their betters deal with matters of state and business. He ought to stick to what he was born to, running machinery, digging coal and putting potatoes in the stew.

Muriel was furious. Shoulders back, head high, she almost marched into the room to challenge the gentlemen. She stopped herself as she placed her hand on the door handle, remembering that she was not in Edinburgh. Here she was just the poor cousin Muriel. In Manchester no one cared a jot over what she thought. In short, she was just a silly woman. She looked away from the chink in the door and caught sight of a maid further down the corridor. The two women met one another's eyes and without needing to speak understood that they had both heard and they both disagreed.

Muriel left the door and moved towards the rear of the house to speak to the maid. As if they were secret agitators, they moved around the back of the staircase.

"Times are changing," the girl spoke, her accent rough like the factory girls Muriel had heard. It was a very different dialect to the one she was used to in Yorkshire, and even from the Scottish of her paternal heritage. "There's new machinery and less work. Them factories update, they say so should society. Country lives off our work, so we should have a voice."

"Who says so? What are they saying?"

"There's a big event coming up, at St Peter's Field. If you're interested you should go."

Before any free time there was an organised itinerary and Moses wanted his wife to come to a factory visit to see how great their own mills would be with the new improvements. Emmerline wasn't particularly interested, but insisted Muriel join them. If she should suffer, so should one and all. In the buildings it was hot and dusty, as if the air was filled with the tiniest particles of cotton. Emmerline felt unwell and hung towards the back of the party. Moses did not notice, too busy marvelling at the spread of machinery, the pace of the weave and the few employees required to keep everything going. Muriel watched her cousin, who clung to her arm, and wondered if she was expecting a second child.

This particular mill was owned by their host, and not that far from where they were staying. They had gone from utter indulgent luxury to the modern powerhouse of mass production. Inside there was floor after floor of looms. The constant clatter of the working machinery and the heat was overbearing, as was the air which felt less than clear. The efficiency of the factories was so great that they would clothe and weave the very air of the room.

"Forty-five horse power steam engine!" The owner, their host and guide, trumpeted as he lead Moses at the head of the group. Muriel, relegated to the back with Emmerline and an assistant who was very well dressed but did not seem to serve any other purpose than to smile at visitors, strained to hear the technical details that the men discussed. With so much noise it was impossible to follow the flow of diagnostics.

The workers, dressed shabbily for their wages would not allow otherwise, were tired but resigned. What energy they had was kept on the job, for to be distracted on shift could mean damaged cloth, loss of wages or even loss of limb. The foreman may well mourn the damage of blood splattered product, but a human less one arm would struggle to find work afterwards and probably die forgotten in a gutter.

The party gathered at one end of the long, endless floor, lit by the smoggy sunlight of outsight. Distracted, Emmerline gazed down the length of the machine to the end closest to them. A petite little girl in a torn smock, with a wan pale face and dark eyes was watching the progress of the machine, regularly darting forward to fix a broken thread. Emmerline could tell by the way she stood and the dexteriority of her fingers that the girl was a few years older than her own little Lydia, yet the girl hardly seemed much taller than Lydia when she tottered about the nursery. She considered the time, and that Lydia would probably be going down for her nap now. This little girl worked as hard and as long as a labourer.

She felt a distress ball up in her stomach and she looked around for someone to explain it away to her. "There are children working here."

The assistant, pleased to feel he was serving a purpose this afternoon, nodded in his finery and darted forward. "That is correct, Mrs Whitfield. We are an important employer of families here and the work keeps the children nimble. The smallest of their hands is very good for fixing broken threads – why, see how she is working here – and the money they earn keeps the family in food. From our side they are very good value for money."

"Because you pay them a pittance," Muriel muttered.

"But they are so small. I don't understand how you can stand to have children working like this." Emmerline sounded close to tears. "Surely they should be outside playing."

"But then they would starve. It is common practice to employ children."

"In your mill?"

"In all the mills."

"All of Manchester sets their children to work? I do not think I care for this city."

Muriel looked aghast at her cousin. "Emmerline, you can't be that stupid, can you?"

"What, are you going to tell me this is acceptable?"

"I don't think so, but I would say someone living off the hard work of children is in no place to cast judgement over an entire city."

"I employ no children."

"Let me assure you that your husband employs more than enough for both of you in the Whitfield mills."

"But he has a daughter," Emmerline started to cry. "I could not bear it for Lydia to be set to work."

You are pregnant, Muriel thought as she gripped her cousin's arm. "Perhaps we should get a little air. Mrs Whitfield is feeling feint."

"Why, yes, of course," The assistant gallantly leapt forward, pointing the way with his polished walking stick as he wrenched open the door. "This way, ladies, I shall soon have you out in the fresh air."

Fresh it was not, but it was marginally cooler, crisper and without the cotton and wool particles drifting into the air passages. They found a little upturned wooden bucket for Emmerline to sit on. The assistant placed a handkerchief across the top lest her skirts be sullied. Emmerline looked as though she was going into shock, and sat hunched forward, worriedly watching children in the distance walking off to work. Muriel was genuinely surprised that her cousin hadn't known that children were employed in Moses' mills. The poor didn't have time for play and schooling. With low wages and high prices, it was all hands to the grindstone if they were going to eat that week. At the opposite end of the spectrum, the rich overindulged, wasted food and sat idle. A cushioned comfort upon the misery of hundreds.

"My dear lady," the assistant broached Emmerline. "Please do not distress yourself. These children are busy and happy. They are bred for it."

"Bred for it? They are not hounds."

"The working classes are a tough breed. They are not the same as you and I; do not carry the same refinement. They are born for hard work and it does them good. For if they were not occupied, they would turn to mischief and drink. You have heard about idle hands?" He laughed, waggling her fingers at her.

Muriel stared at the back of his head in disgust. How could someone apparently so well educated be so intensely stupid? All were born equal, fragile and innocent babes and it was mere chance of the situation one was born into whether one would own a mill or slave away one's short years within. She felt an urge to strike him, but suppressed it. This was the conservative upper class and none of them was going to listen to an unmarried eccentric woman. They would mark it down as hysteria and nothing more.

"I think my cousin has one of her headaches," she said, catching Emmerline's eye who nodded her consent. "Could you possibly arrange a carriage to take us back to our apartments?"

He jumped up, joyful to the task and smiled. "It would be my pleasure." And off he ran, the willing little dog.

Emmerline wiped at her eyes. "I did not know," she cried at Muriel. "I keep thinking of the hollow look on that girl's face. There was nothing there. Hope extinguished before she had started. I did not know. And you say it is like this in other places?"

"It's like this everywhere. Life is cheap." Muriel held out her hand. "Let's get away from this place. I've lost my interest in new technology just now. Let's go see Lydia."

"Yes." Emmerline brightened a little. "I'd like to see my little girl."

That Monday was a particularly fine day. In places other than Manchester the sun may well have fully washed the earth. However, in the hub of the industrial revolution there was always a certain level of smog in the city. Despite the soots, one could feel it was a fine day.

Summer and sun usually made her joyful but Emmerline was on edge. She filled with regret as she followed Muriel and Agnes Learie, one of the maids from the apartments, down Quay Street. She ought to have stayed at home and played with Lydia. She ought to have remained in her own fine clothes rather than being persuaded to wear Muriel's second shabbiest outfit and leave all her jewels on the dressing table. The maid had tied her hair back in a very simple and regular fashion, and when Emmerline caught sight of herself in the mirror she could have been a factory girl in her Sunday best. That had caught the maid off guard, who had laughed, forgetting her place, and made a comment that no factory woman had hands like hers. Emmerline wasn't sure if she was more upset by how obvious her naiveté was, or that she had taken the jump from girl to woman without even noticing.

She paused a moment to look up at a poster advertising this event for the working man. Muriel had been talking with the maids under the staircase, and had been planning to attend as soon as she had caught wind of it. Originally the meet had been planned for a week ago, but there had been something about the itinerary that had made the magistrates hot under the collar and declare it illegal. Carefully reworded it was all right to go ahead, but it seemed a mere technicality if everyone was intending to do exactly what they would have done the other week.

If they hadn't joined her husband on the factory visit and Emmerline hadn't reacted so badly to the sight of little children working long hours and so obviously suffering for it, perhaps Muriel wouldn't have been so adamant that her cousin was to join them on the outing. Emmerline had lived in her upper class bubble too long, full of notions that the working man was a different species, and that the French revolution part deux on English soil was only around the corner and must be squashed. Emmerline protested she had never thought such a thing, those were her husband's opinions and she was quite capable of thinking for herself. Exactly, Muriel had agreed, snapping her fingers. And that was why Emmerline had to come and listen to the fabulous Henry Hunt.

"And you're sure there's not going to be any trouble?" Emmerline asked, noting yet another shop boarded up. She hurried to catch up with the other women.

"Not a jot, we're not savages, you know," Agnes retorted. "Besides, Mr Hunt says no one's to bring any kind of a weapon. We're above such behaviour. We're members of society and we know how to behave."

There were a lot of people out on the streets, all in their Sunday best, women with flowers pinned to their jackets, children with scrubbed little faces. Indeed there was an atmosphere of a fair, an excitement in the air, and distant music. Something great would be seen this afternoon. They headed towards St Peter's Field, an open rough area surrounded by buildings, mills and church spires. Already a lot of people had gathered, as if the entire city had just poured into one little clean bubble of land in amongst all of the industry. Emmerline felt a little overwhelmed. She'd spent part of her childhood in Leeds, then York, then abroad, and had enjoyed some holidays out in the countryside in the old family home at Commondale. She'd lived in big centres of population yet she had never been with so many people at once, not even at some of the balls she had attended. Emmerline's world was big roomy properties and fine houses, statements of space of value. She gazed across the field to a row of properties with windows overlooking the fields. Would there be people inside, watching this amazing spectacle and wondering what it would all come to?

Bands of people continued to arrive. Agnes had told them that workers were coming from all over Lancashire to hear Mr Hunt speak, such a great man as he was. Groups marched in carrying banners with slogans such as 'Liberty' and one group of women carried one stating ' Let us die like men, and not be sold like slaves'. There were people of all ages, even children, who were probably enjoying a day off work. Today they were out with their mothers and siblings, enjoying the sunshine and being told that this man was going to make life better for them. In one corner a hustings had been built from a couple of carts and planks of wood positioned over the top to create a stage. Seemingly hundreds of special constables loitered in the area.

"Here's a fine trio of Lancashire Witches!"

The three women turned to find a couple of Manchester lads dofting their caps at them as they strolled through the crowds. Agnes immediately put her hand to her mouth and tittered. Emmerline stretched herself up very tall, aghast at the incorrect nature of their statement. "I'm not from Lancashire." She proclaimed which set off laughter in all parties.

Agnes watched the lads stroll on before turning back to her two guests. "They just mean we're pretty, silly."

"Agnes, my lass." A young man slipped out from the surrounding milling masses. "Good to see you came."

"Oh, Jimmy," she gasped, her hands reaching out for his sleeves. "I wouldn't have missed it for the world."

"And you've brought more recruits with you, I see," he nodded approvingly.

"Oh yes, this is Miss Muriel and Miss Emmerline."

"Nice to make your acquaintance," he dofted his cap to them. "Might I take Agnes a moment to meet a few friends?" And with that she was whisked back into the mêlée, never to be seen again that day.

"Miss Emmerline?" she hissed at her cousin. "I am a married lady."

"You're playing a role whilst you're here," Muriel reminded her.

"I don't see why I need to be here."

"Because this is history being made. I told you what they're fighting for. This country will become great."

"Votes for all?" Emmerline muttered sarcastically.

"That and fair representation. These people are crippled by taxes and don't have enough to eat, they can't afford the food. Yet they don't own land so they can't vote and even if they could, there are not enough MPs to represent the number of people. Then there are corrupt boroughs where no one lives, yet two MPs, fat, out-of-touch landowners, are sent to represent the grass and the rocks. It's not right."

"It's nothing to do with us."

"What, because you are rich?"

Emmerline stared at her cousin. Muriel was fired up. Emmerline could understand why more than just people like her husband, who was quite an idiot, should be allowed to vote, likewise that they ought to have the members of parliament proportional to where the people of the country was. If the government wanted to take tax from people and rule over their lives, in turn people ought to have the right to pick who would be in such a government. But the fire in Muriel's eyes suggested she directly would benefit. In fact, there were so many women here, Emmerline wondered if someone had neglected to point out the finer details to a lot of them. "They're only talking about votes for men. Nobody cares what we think. Nobody wants us involved."

Muriel had been imagining voting as Kaarel Must, even though she had no plans of attempting her university career again. She looked to Emmerline. "Well, it's a start, isn't it?"

"I suppose. I just wonder how many would turn up if we were shouting for votes for women."

A cheer went up across the way and a cart followed by yet another parade of people entered the fray. The underlying buzz of hope and excitement heightened. It was Henry Hunt, accompanied by a well dressed woman on the cart. He stood up, waving his white hat, and the sea of people cheered and waved their hands in response. Emmerline looked from the speaker who was making his way to the stage, to other corners of the field and all she could see was people. There must be thousands packed into this green space. She stepped up a little closer to Muriel. "We must not lose one another here."

"Don't worry," Muriel told her. "Nothing bad will happen to you here."

Henry Hunt alighted the stage and stood in silence for some time surveying the crowd. Perhaps he was surprised by just how many people had come to hear him speak. It was so packed with people now that Emmerline could not see an exit line for even a couple of metres had she wished to leave. She watched as some more gentlemen joined Mr Hunt on the stage, along with some women – how odd, she thought, are they going to add votes for women to the list of demands? – and some other men whose heads were up and down like chickens, alternating between gazing at proceedings and ducking to scribble down their thoughts in notebooks. Journalists were to account for the speech in order to report back to those who could not attend and probably most of the crowd who wouldn't hear the speech.

Henry Hunt held up his hands for attention, as if he did not already have the crowd's full attention, and began to speak. Emmerline and Muriel were quite a distance from the hustings and although they could hear his voice they could not quite make out the words. A man just ahead of them had better hearing, and in bursts was whispering the gist to his wife, who in turn bent down to inform the children.

"Mr Hunt says thank you for coming."

"Mr Hunt says to keep order and restrain anyone who tries to make trouble."

"Does he mean me, Ma?" asked the little lad.

"No love, proper trouble makers who do not care for what we are here to do."

Mr Hunt continued to give his eager speech, hat in one hand, the other punching the air to deliver each point and demand he had to make. An uneasy electricity started to move through the crowds, sparking from one person to another and spreading like fire. Muriel thought she heard someone cry 'the soldiers', but they were packed in by a sea of bodies and she couldn't see anything that even looked like a soldier. Emmerline gripped her forearm with both hands. "A two year old has just been trampled to death."

Muriel looked in horror at her cousin. "What are you talking about?" she whispered furiously, hoping no one else had heard. In such a tightly packed crowd, panic could be fatal.

"Look," Emmerline pointed. Muriel followed her line of direction. Across from the hustings, from the corner of the field, cavalry soldiers were entering the crowds. The people on the stage were already aware of the arrival, and Hunt was shouting at people to remain calm and give a big cheer for the cavalry. In response the crowd started to boo and hiss. The horses, well trained but nevertheless agitated by such noise and volume moved onwards at an inappropriately fast speed whilst their riders brandished sabres above their heads. Hunt continued to try and calm the situation, although not enough could hear him. The cavalry wanted to get to him and the hustings, for there were arrests to be made. Progress was not being made quickly enough. A scream went up, the sabres went down slashing and the cavalry charged towards the hustings, cutting at whoever did not get out of the way quickly enough.

A sickened panic swept through the crowds and people started to look to their own, darting here and there to try and get away, but the sheer volume of people stopped them. The cavalry made it to the hustings and gestured to Hunt, who said something back, but did not move until another couple of men came onto the hustings shaking papers – perhaps warrants for arrest, and Hunt and another man were taken down from the stage. The cavalry surrounded the stage and banners began to be torn down. The special constables were swarming at the stage and seemingly going for the female reformers, who, all dressed in white, stood out like glowing targets. The children in front of Muriel and Emmerline were crying now and clinging to their mother's skirts. No one knew what to do. Many were shouting abuse, others looked like they wanted to run away, but there was so much confusion a body couldn't get anywhere. The cavalry were turning on the people close by who were shouting at them. Blood flowed. A woman clutching her baby was slashed across the head, her baby drenched in its mother's blood. Screams and curses filled the air, and the dust from the ground rose as the mass body of people tried to run in every direction all at once.

Muriel and Emmerline clung to one another, disorientated and ignorant to the geography of Manchester. The air was thick with screams and blood, and Muriel's eyes welled up with tears of panic. She was not able to cope with this. It was just like the operation in Edinburgh, watching the screaming woman on the table and running away.

Suddenly a soldier on foot burst out of the writhing bodies, brandishing his bayonet and slashing wildly. The foot soldiers had been sent into the crowds, only to be overwhelmed by sheer numbers, separated and packed in. The man was panicking and slashed without looking. A sharp, infant scream went up as his blade hacked at the little boy's arm, he who had been stood just in front of Muriel and Emmerline. The mother flung herself onto her child as the soldier stared dumbly at what he was done. "Have mercy on me," he wailed before he was sucked back into the crowds. A stone flew overhead.

Blood gushed out of the boy's arm. The wounded arm hung lifelessly. His childish face was suddenly very old and weary, growing pale. Muriel ducked down to the ground, ripping at petticoats as she went, and set herself at the feet of the patient.

"Oh lord, can you help him?" the mother wailed.

Jostled on the ground, she had to work fast before they were trampled underfoot. The cavalry were now setting up to charge in and rescue the infantry and clear the field. It already felt as though the density of the crowds was thinning, and it was possible to see routes out. Shoes and hats, bloodied bonnets and torn shards of clothes lay upon the dusty ground. Muriel ignored it all. Looking at the damage of the little arm, the soft childish skin now torn and bloodied. It looked as though the bone was chipped, but not broken – for the wound was so deep she could see the bone – and could be saved. She swiftly bound up the wound, until the upper arm was completely bandaged, and tightened as much as she could. A bloom of blood rushed through the white cotton. Muriel looked at the woman. "This is only temporary. It needs to be stitched."

"We don't have the money for things like that."

Emmerline clung to Muriel's side. "We have to get out of here."

People fleeing the scene bumped into the cluster. The boy's pallor did not look good. A sticky sheen was beading across his skin. Muriel put her arms under him and looked at the mother. "You know Manchester? You can guide us to where we need to go."

"I'll take you anywhere."

"We'll go to the kitchens, I'll fix him there."

"We can't all go to the apartments," Emmerline gasped.

"We'll go through the service entrance." Muriel stood up.

"But what will the servants say?"

"Servants?" the woman gasped.

"We have to go now."

The woman and Emmerline held on to Muriel, the red-headed, bold woman leading the way as they fled the field. The boy became an ever more heavy weight in Muriel's arms. She hoped that she would not fail. They neared an exit out onto a street and slowed. It was a bottle neck where people were trying to escape whilst cavalry men hacked at them. An officer rode up shouting in fury and knocking back their sabres out of harm's way with his own metal. "Let these people pass, damn it!"

Caught up in the swell of people, like a storm-driven tidal swell sweeping up out of the harbour, the little bloodied group were pushed out of St Peter's Field, such a holy name for such an unholy occurrence, and thrown forth into the streets of Manchester. It had felt like hours, but perhaps in ten minutes the field was cleared, save the military, the dead and the groaning wounded, the bloodied pools and torn clothing. A sickening shock at what had happened, or in some quarters a great pride at an enemy defeated, soaked through the city.

"You were quite amazing," Emmerline had told her cousin in all seriousness, when the woman and her young son had left the property via the trade entrance. "If you were not a woman, I would be quite convinced you were a professional doctor."

The kitchen staff had been more than a little surprised when the mismatched group had stumbled in the back way, wide-eyed and blood splashed with a child that looked like death. All three women were dishevelled and out of breath, only Muriel still with a hat on her head. She had commanded the situation, and with a level headed cook who had gotten the scullery maid's mind off gawking and back on the fetching, Muriel soon had her makeshift operating kit laid out. She had focused on her work, asked the cook to hold the boy, and stitched up the wound. She had ignored his cries, for it was more important to get it properly stitched up before he lost any more blood. She instructed the mother on changing the bandages, what to look for, and at what point she would have to call for a doctor, due to risk of infection. She had even given the woman a doctor's fee so that she should not hesitate if the need arose, but suspected that money would go straight on to food for the entire family. Agnes, the maid and their guide to the protest had returned just as the mother and son were leaving. The two unacquainted women had exchanged stories for a few minutes. The cook listened in, crossing herself and shaking her head at what the world was come to, before the ladies of the house slipped through to the other side.

They had managed to creep into their rooms unnoticed and Muriel was sure they had gotten away with their little outing. Someone had told, passing gossip from downstairs to upstairs. Later in the evening Moses had turned up, drunk and furious. Emmerline had embarrassed him by dancing off with those radicals and working class people. They were beneath their social standing. What was worse, those fools had no sense or right to be asking what they demanded. The afternoon's descent into thuggery had only proved what a bunch of ignorant pugilists they were. They had started a riot. Emmerline began to protest that the current state of the country was not just. Children should not be working in the factories. People should be fairly paid. It was not the protestors who had started the riot, rather the cavalry. Moses had slapped her and told her to watch her tongue. She was just a woman and she did not know what she spoke of. Despite the smarting red cheek she had tried to explain that people with money such as theirs had a duty. He had all out hit her in the face, the force of which had thrown her across the bed. She should respect the opinion of her betters and not try to correct them. She had no money. Everything was his, and with good reason the law of the land made it so. That included Lydia, so she had better become a better wife and forget all this radical nonsense. Spies from France, trying to destroy an Englishman's good fortune. And that stupid cousin of hers, too boyish and ugly to get a man, perhaps she really was a man. She'd suck up such nonsense as all this. There'd be no more socialising with her strange family, they were a bad influence. In fact Muriel would not accompany them to Buxton, she could get out now and go back to that witch mother of hers in her witch hovel in the hills. That was how Muriel came to have a red faced, shouting arse enter her room and advise her to get her bags packed, for she was going home at first light.

Muriel had been awake and already mentally packing. She had decided she would not attend Buxton, for she needed to get back to Haworth and then onwards to York as soon as possible. She had operated on a patient, when the moment came she had been ready. That was why she needed to be a doctor. She would complete her transformation into Mr Must at her sister's apartments, then get herself back up to Edinburgh to complete her studies.

That autumn she was back at Edinburgh to restart her studies. Erskine MacKenzie was just starting his final year of study, and was pleasantly surprised to find his old friend Kaarel Must back after over a year of no communication. He tried to draw some semblance of an answer from Must as to where he had been and what had happened, but without success.

In fact Kaarel was just as silent on personal matters as Muriel had been. After a month back at home in Haworth with her mother, she packed up her belongings and departed, saying she had things to do. Eleanor did not hear from her daughter for the next six months. And so her family disappeared. Her sons were long dead these years past, her eldest daughter Elizabeth she had not heard from since she had last seen her in Scarborough many years ago, and now Muriel behaved as though she wanted nothing more to do with their connection. Yet there had been no angry words, no finality, only a slipping away. Eleanor received letters from her niece, Emmerline, trying to locate Muriel, so she ought to find some solace in the fact the whole family had been cut off but it was of little help. Neither was the fact that Emmerline's husband did not wish her to consort with her poorer relatives anymore, so the letters had to be sent via a servant's family home. Emmerline confided that she and Muriel had attended the Peterloo – as it was now being referred to – rally, something which had not helped family relations. Eleanor had read about the rally, the subsequent events and all the related debate in the newspapers. She had noted that the organisers were currently under arrest due to be tried at the next York assizes. She lay down the paper and leant back into her chair. The York assizes, when the judges next came to the town and tried all the prisoners who were languishing in the prison. The last time she had attended those she had witnessed the trial and execution of her younger sister, Emmerline's mother. Clara had been dead ten years now. It was strange. It felt like only yesterday, and yet at the same time something so distant as to be an event she had read in a book or almost imaged. One could almost fool oneself into thinking that person had never really existed.

The winter was dark, cold and long and people stayed in their houses as much as possible, only coming out for work or to buy supplies. The time passed. Spring arrived, Eleanor received a note to announce the birth of Emmerline's second daughter, Charity, and in the warming sunshine she could almost believe in new hope were it not for the arrival of a distraught Temperance Heaton at her back door. The young woman was grey, wan and clutching the limp, bony little body of her dead baby. There was no money for a funeral. Mrs Heaton, her mother-in-law, had told her to keep up with the funeral insurance, but Temperance had chosen to try and feed her children instead. Her husband had gotten involved in the trade union movement, protesting for better rights and the vote for all men, and had found himself in trouble, and out of a job. Prices continued to rise, damn the Corn Laws he would say, whilst ranting about the political injustices, but words were not putting food in their bellies and the family grew thinner and weaker. When the baby died, only last night, her husband had gone to pieces and disappeared. She had taken the elder child to her mother-in-law whilst she went to plead for the baby's soul and a decent burial but the reverend was unable to help. She had just been at the parochial house and had been staggering aimlessly before remembering Eleanor MacCaskill.

Anne Thwaite, the housekeeper, hovered in the shadows near the doorway and gave Eleanor a look as if to say she ought to send the girl on her way. Eleanor did not know what to do. She did not know this girl, indeed she had only briefly helped her in delivering a letter to her sweetheart. It had been a seemingly innocent deed that had put the father's curses and damnation upon them. Thankfully even he had grown bored of the stalking and dark stares in the last year.

"You could not ask your father..."

"My father will not speak to me," Temperance wailed. "He would see a child of mine thrown to the pigs for fodder. He has told me so. But look at him." She thrust the little bundle of rags, in which a stiffened, malnourished three month old lay crumpled. "He's done nothing wrong and they will not bury him without the money."

Eleanor looked at the body and regretted it. All babies look so similar when they are little, although admittedly this one was more bone and skin than her little ones had been. But it reminded her of her own children, and how innocent and trusting they had been. Out in a strange world and implicitly needing to rely on these big people to provide everything. So that they might grow and experience life and thought.

Temperance started coughing and wobbled as if she were about to collapse. The smell emanating from her dirty, ragged dress was not pleasant. It had started to rain outside as well, just to add to the hopelessness of the scene, and the young woman's hair was flattened against her scalp.

"I don't know what to do."

"Perhaps you should come in and warm yourself by the fire."

Anne Thwaite tutted and stomped off to the kitchen, but Eleanor knew that she would warm up some water and make sure the girl was clean and free of infestation before she left.

"Where are you living?"

"Just a dirty cellar. We can't afford much now Daniel does not work." She dropped onto a little stool by the fire and clutched the baby to her. "It's awful. It's always wet and damp and dreadful horrid in the winter. The air is stale and we hear the neighbours. The girls crying at night. The shouting." She looked into the fire. "One of the girls has got herself in the family way they say. Father's thrown her out of the room they all live in. She's only thirteen. And tis a sin as he's the one who did it."

"Mrs Heaton, one should not spread such rumours and tales!" Anne burst out.

"We all know it's true. And they're not the only family to treat the daughters like that. Tis a den of misery. There is no life or hope. Only work for starvation and early death. I know why my Daniel is so angry and so wishes for change but oh, I wish we could..." She looked down at her little bundle of rags. "His mother said not to get attached till they were five."

"I will go and speak to the new reverend," Eleanor said. "They seem like a decent family."

She hoped that it was simply the smell and state of Temperance that had temporarily interrupted their charitable nature, but upon entering the house she did have to wonder. The Reverend Bronte was not there, but she spoke to his wife, who was very familiar with the case, having only just seen Temperance an hour earlier.

"And she is some relation of yours?"

"Relation. No, why, I..."

"Oh. Only there is a similar look between you."

"She is just a local girl I have known for some years. But she is distraught. Her child has just died. A mere babe."

The woman, Maria Bronte, a slight little creature with curls and an angelic countenance, nodded sadly. "I know. The same age as my little Anne. It is very sad. I understand the circumstances of the poor in Haworth to be very hard. That this is happening a lot. God's way is a hard path."

She's going to spin me the line that we can't save everyone and send me on my way, Eleanor thought. "I realise you will hear pleas of charity like this daily, but could not an exception be made. This girl has not had an easy life and she is devastated."

The woman nodded distractedly, winced and put her hand to her lower abdomen. "Mrs MacCaskill, I understand you are a mother as well. I believe we women feel more, and as mothers we project another's tragedy into our own circumstances. But it's easy to forget we are a different class and we feel more keenly." She gripped Eleanor's wrist, and her fingers dug into the flesh in time with another wince. "I would try to look at it all in a different light. The poverty can be a blessing. It keeps them from sin. They are simple folk, very open to the bible and she will find solace there."

"What is this nonsense?"

Maria's eyes widened a little. "A godly thought and not nonsense. I had heard you were a little outspoken..."

"What about the dead baby. The babe the same age as your Anne."

"They do not have money, any money, and we have our own..." she paused. "Mrs MacCaskill, you must excuse me."

The woman was doubled over in pain now. Although Eleanor could have shook her for some of the nonsense she had started to spout, she was not unfeeling, and took the woman's arm. "Let me help you to a chair. You do not look well."

"Thank you. This was my sixth child and I ought to be used to it, but I do declare it is a little harder in the recovery after every one of them."

"I do not wish to trouble you further. You look as though you need rest. I am leaving the fee here," she added, putting some coins on the table. "Temperance will stay with me until this matter is complete. If you could ask your husband to contact me when he returns home, I would be most grateful." She moved to stand up and heard a little cough from the corridor. Eleanor paused and glanced over her shoulder to see a rather stern and doll sized little girl watching them.

Maria caught sight of the child. "Charlotte," she said. "Do go back to your sisters."

The girl lingered in the doorway for a moment or two and boldly stared Eleanor directly in the eye. Without a word, she turned and disappeared into the shadows of the corridor.

With the payment, the funeral for the little child, thankfully already baptised, was completed. Eleanor was not sure if the new Reverend Bronte truly would have turned Temperance away without payment, but it was no matter. The baby was buried, but the ceremony brought no solace to Temperance. Her husband, Daniel Heaton, looked like an empty shell as he watched his child interred in the earth. Supposedly to find peace and be with God, yet it felt like such an utter waste of potential. Eleanor stood at the graveside and cried for them. So young and too poor to love this much. It was a catalyst to more heartbreak than any one soul could carry. He and Temperance could barely look at one another, for what their marriage had wreaked. No sooner was the ceremony over than he was back to travelling. No one locally would employ him, so he was working further afield up in the Dales at a quarry. He still had a wife and one daughter to support, even though he could not quite face them yet. If he had been of logical and calm mind, he would have thought to take them with him, for the air and water was better in the hills where he worked, but he could not find a way out of the fog of his grief.

The little girl was still with her mother-in-law, but Temperance made no attempt to fetch her. She was numb and lost in her own mind. She knelt by the grave and was unable to move. Her mother-in-law, constrained by a band of other little ones, was unable and truth be told unwilling to help, and left her. Temperance's own family had not attended. There was no one. So Eleanor took her home, another faltering mind to add to the collection, for Maud was very vague these days. Temperance sat by the fire in the kitchen and did nothing. Anne Thwaite shook her head and muttered something about a distraction from Muriel, but understood that her mistress was a kind-hearted woman and Temperance was too stunned by life to contemplate taking advantage. After a few days, she wondered what the longer term plan might be on the part of either woman, but that night Temperance delivered her solution to the limbo with a rather drastic decision.

Although she left the house in the night, they did not realise until the following morning. Maud had woken promptly and gone to her window to gaze out on the moorland of her childhood. There was something in the copse of trees that did not look right, and she called out for her daughters Eleanor and Gillian. Only Eleanor answered. There was something dislodged from the branches. Perhaps a bough had broken? It looked wrong. She did not remember it that way.

Anne Thwaite and Eleanor ran out and got Temperance down. A lonely creak swung from the trees and went a wandering out across the moors. She was cold and stiff and her spirit was long gone. They could only hope she had found some peace, but it looked as though it had been a miserable and violent death. Both women were red faced and out of breath when they had finally gotten Temperance down from her place of self execution. Eleanor stumbled backwards as she lost her balance, landing bottom first in the heather, with her arms still locked under Temperance's armpits.

Anne and Eleanor stared at one another in silence for a good few minutes, waiting for their pulses to return to a steady level. What was there to be said? It was a sorry, tragic doing, and there were thousands more than Temperance who had lost babies. Hundreds of thousands who lived in squalid conditions and had no hope.

The housekeeper was the first to break the silence. "He'll not bury her."

Eleanor was about to protest that she would pay whatever was necessary, then realised what Anne was referring to. Suicide was an ungodly act. "We'll take her home, wash and prepare the body." She gazed down at the ugly bruising around the neck. "A high collar would be in order."

"I could say I found her in bed."

"She died of grief," Eleanor colluded.

"People down there drop like flies," Anne muttered, referring to the lower end of the town.

"Exactly, and many don't have such acute heartaches. Muriel always said the water down there was rancid." Eleanor bit her lip at the casual mention of her missing daughter. She found herself hugging Temperance's corpse.

Anne sent word out to Mrs Heaton, Daniel Heaton and also up to Top Hail Farm, whilst Eleanor took the task of returning to the parsonage to ask for another funeral. Mrs Heaton said she was not surprised, Temperance had struggled with town living; and Daniel sent word that he was coming. Not a word came from Top Hail.

"Has he been told that his only daughter is dead?" Eleanor snapped angrily, marching out of the parlour where they had to keep Temperance's body in readiness for the burial. "I cannot believe a parent would be so callous as to carry a grudge to death."

Anne Thwaite pursed her lips. "He knows. I sent a lad up there myself. And I've seen Netty, his housekeeper."

"And what did he say? Did he not shed a tear?"

Anne shook her head. Horace Denver was beyond saving. "He spat and said good riddance, if you must know. That is a bad man up there, he's not worth troubling over."

"And what about her brother, Abraham?"

"He does as he is told."

"So she is to have no kin to see her into the next life?"

"Please calm yourself," Anne begged, a little shocked by Eleanor's furious reaction. The girl's death grieved her more than she had expected, but she was still certain that some of this was fall out from Muriel's desertion. "They are not good people and we must accept that nothing can be done."

Eleanor glowered at the fire. So they would sit up there, isolated in high judgement and be excused from facing the consequences of their actions. Daniel arrived soon after, a hollow ghost. She left him with the body of his wife.

Slinging her husband's old drover's coat around her shoulders, Eleanor set out onto the moors. Her anger pushed her forwards and made her muscles blind to the incline as she marched. Heather tugged and scratched at her skirts as she covered the landscape, heading directly for her target some miles south west.

The farmstead was shut up for the evening when she arrived, but she could see the chinks of light from the windows. Any attempt at negotiation or a polite arrival were cast aside, and she was straight at the door hammering and shouting. "You devil-spawn. How dare you not honour your daughter. You let her die and even now you ignore her."

The house stared upon her in disapproving silence.

Eleanor took a step back from the door. "Will you not answer me? Are you afraid, Horace Denver? Are you not ashamed?"

The door was abruptly wrenched open, making Eleanor involuntarily jump back. The master of the house, looking ever more the wild beast of the moors, loomed out from the shadows. "You be gone from my property, you mad banshee. I'll not have you screaming your woman's nonsense..."

"Your daughter is dead."

"I have no daughter."

"Temperance is dead."

"A curse be on you. And a curse be on her. She had no respect."

"She will be buried tomorrow and her kin should be there."

"I'll not weep at her grave. Her kin will be there."

"Her mother-in-law and her husband will be there, but I'm talking about her blood."

"So am I." He looked as though he were about to spit in her general direction but thought better of it. "You Feathers have always been bad omens for my people. Your mother thought she'd get her feet under the table, after my old dead uncle."

"You're talking about Samuel Denver?"

"That's the one, my father's mirror image. The family made sure they pried her claws out. I was only a lad at the time but I remember. A wanton whore. She got Samuel to fill her belly. He always was a fool for a pretty stare. We got her thrown out and she ought to have died in the gutter, but that travelling merchant took her on. Ugly little runt he was. And a fool with it to take her with another man's child." He paused and looked at her cunningly. "Although I heard it was twins, two of them, like my father and Samuel. I heard your sister got hung. Paid for your blood's shame."

"You evil old bastard; don't you talk about my sister. May you rot in hell."

Horace laughed a deep roar from the belly of damnation. "We do share some blood, for you can curse when you wish."

"How dare you..."

"Get away with you, damned wench," he waved her off with an idle hand. "Before I set the dogs on you. I'll have no more to do with your people." And with that final statement he slammed the door in her face.

Eleanor spat at the ground. "May you pay for your sins, Horace Denver. You will be sorry." She turned and started on a fast walk to get away from Top Hail. She managed a few hundred metres before she had to drop to her knees and throw up in the heather. This meant that she and Horace Denver were cousins and shared blood. It was the final recognition of who her father actually had been. An uplands farmer by the name of Samuel Denver. She did not come from goblin stock of the Hursts, but from the devil instead. Temperance had been her first cousin once removed, and neither had known of the connection. Muriel had been her second cousin, had she been in contact with her family, Eleanor could have written to her. She started to cry. Why had her daughters abandoned her in this way and refused all communication? She had always tried her best for them, to give them good lives and opportunities. She had wanted to protect them. She had not done anything so terrible as to warrant this silence.

Old superstitions dictate that occurrences of a particular nature always happen in groups of three. Another death was due. A wide-eyed Netty had hobbled across the moors to buy supplies in town, and spread her eyewitness news wherever she went, which was how the MacCaskills learned of it. Eleanor's homestead was one of the first Netty reached as she came down from the wild moors. Besides, Netty always liked to stop by and see Anne Thwaite. Usually it was to catch up on the gossip from Anne so that she could chatter with the best of them when she got into town, but those days it was Netty who was full of the most shocking of tales.

The first day she was on an early mission to fetch a doctor. There was something wrong with the master. He had been in a foul mood ever since the news of Temperance's death, sleeping less and less and taking to walking out on the moors in the moonlight, cursing the very wind that pushed back at him. Netty had arrived that morning to find Abraham running about the yard, jabbering that his father had not been out nor to bed that night but merely sat at the table and glared at the fire. He was still there and Abraham could get no sense from him. It was as if the furious body remained but the mind and the sense had departed for a walk and neglected to return. Yet the man was most definitely not dead.

The doctor made the journey on horseback that morning, and took only a few minutes to examine the patient, declaring it to be a very intense attack of apoplexy. And never was a term more fitting, commented the doctor, who was well acquainted with Horace's reputation. "To be struck down with violence," he told Netty. "That is the literal translation from the Greek."

"To be sure, I don't know what the Greeks had to do with it all," Netty said to Anne later on.

"He has had an intense and violent bleed in the brain," the doctor explained, seeing that Netty did not understand in the slightest. "That is why he neither speaks nor moves. His mind is severely wounded."

"And will he recover?"

"Every case is different. Many do to a greater or lesser extent. But that he does not move or react at all..." The doctor straightened. "There is little we can do for him but give it time. Let me know if his condition changes."

Listening to the story some days later, Anne tutted at the account of the doctor's words.

"What was I to do?" Netty asked. "The lad is less than useless. So I stayed overnight for the last few days. I do confess when he started to talk, I thought we were out of danger and he would soon be his old swearing self again. But it were very odd. He'd have long conversations and look about, but at things we couldn't see or hear."

"His mind was permanently cracked."

"Indeed. Then three mornings after we'd first found him without his wits about him, we found him dead. Stone cold, eyes open and glaring at the fire. I could not get that look of anger off his face. He was quite a shock to put in a coffin."

And so there was a third funeral to attend. It was paid for by the surprising amount of coin squirreled away at Top Hail Farm. Few attended. Abraham, a couple of farm workers and Netty Duncombe were the only ones at the front who made any attempt of attending for the sake of the deceased. A few curious locals hung about in the graveyard to see the conclusion of a very odd little drama. Eleanor hung in the background, but showed her face at the ceremony. She had learned the full truth of her parentage, and yet gained nothing from it. Nothing positive had been added to her family tree, merely a collection of dead relatives, some of them intensely hateful. She had always assumed nothing could be worse than the parentage of Hobart Hurst. The Denvers were certainly a group to put up some serious competition. What was one to think about the fact that one had come from such a cold bed of misery?

Eleanor could be forgiven for thinking that Horace's death closed the chapter on her paternal family history. The following year an appendix was included. Mrs Heaton, over-worked and humourless mother to Temperance's now widower husband, Daniel, appeared at the back door with a small entourage of her younger children about her. In the crook of one arm she carried a wicker basket, in the other a baby of four or five months wrapped up in grubby, worn swaddling clothes that had seen many a babe before. A six year old girl and a three year old girl loitered silent and grim faced around her skirts. Both were scrawny creatures, but well attired in worn, thinning dresses and bonnets. Mrs Heaton did the best she could with the money and facilities at her disposal, and no one would say her children were not attended to.

Faces washed in icy cold, grimy water stared accusingly at Eleanor, as if to ask what right she had in living in such clean and fresh rooms, when they scrabbled about in dank, dreary tenement cells for their brief childhood. If they survived it, they'd soon be off to the mills or mines for work, for mouths needed food the family could not afford.

Mrs Heaton raised her chin in defiance. Just anyone try and call her poor.

"Mrs Heaton," Eleanor pushed the door wide open, non-plussed to find the woman at her house. From her position in the doorway she could see back into the kitchen, where Anne Thwaite had ceased kneading the bread, unashamedly listening to this unexpected visit. Mrs Heaton was unable to see Anne from the threshold.

"My Daniel is still working at the quarry up in the Dales."

"That is... very good." What did the woman want? "To have steady and rewarding employment..."

"He's had a very hard year," Mrs Heaton interrupted, not interested in Mrs MacCaskill's idle wanderings. As if rewarding had anything to do with a job, unless it meant one could pay the rent and feed the children. No one went to work for enjoyment. "What with Temperance and the baby dying. It's been very hard on him. I always said it would come to a bad end getting embroiled with that Top Hail lot, but what's done is done."

They all stood at the doorway in silence.

"The point is," Mrs Heaton abruptly continued. "He's starting to make a new life for himself. He won't come back to Haworth for it saddens him so. But he has good lodgings and is getting on at the quarry, like. And he's met a good woman up there. They're to be married. He deserves it. A chance to have something. Start fresh. He doesn't want any reminders of that sad time. No hangers on. Doesn't want any baggage from the past."

"I..."

"Problem is, me and my husband, what with food prices ever going up, we struggle. We struggle for the food and the rent and forgive my language, but it is a sad little hole we live in, without the space enough for a family of rats, let alone people." She eyed the corridor Eleanor stood in as if that was point enough and explained the end goal of her visit. All that space, and only Eleanor MacCaskill and her confused aged mother in permanent residence. It was a disgrace.

"I had thought I would have to go to one of them foundlings places..."

Eleanor had one eye on the kitchen. It dawned on her why Mrs Heaton was here. From the way Anne Thwaite thumped her fists into the dough it was clear she had also realised what Mrs Heaton wanted. Nay, what she was about to do regardless of anyone else's opinion. Eleanor stared at the three year old girl who was fixedly staring at her thick stocking feet (no shoes), being bold and pretending the streaks of tears weren't clearing the grime off her sallow cheeks.

"Kin ought to be with kin when money allows. But we have less than none and my Daniel will have his fresh start. As I say, I was going to a home for foundlings, and then I remembered what folk round here say. The stories of your mother and Samuel Denver. Truth be known, you look like the Denvers, although I'll grant you a better temperament and a decency about you. I know you paid for both the babe and Temperance to be properly buried. So you're as much kin as I am. This is Jayne." She roughly stuck her hand in between the little girl's shoulder blades and pushed her forward.

Eleanor couldn't take her eyes off the little girl. She was a little too short for a three year old, and so thin. Her bonnet was limp about her face, her dark hair creeping loose. I am fifty eight years old, Eleanor thought; I am too old for the rearing of children.

"I appreciate you're an older woman of course, and no one is under any obligation. If it is too much, or simply not required, there is always the foundling home." She gave Eleanor a curt nod. "I'll say good day to you." And with that, she turned to go, both children moving to follow until a glare from the elder girl halted the younger. The Heatons proper left and the three year old lingered on the exterior doorstep.

Eleanor put a hand to her forehead. This was the last thing she had been expecting.

"Am I to go to the foundlings to be eaten by dogs?" The little girl spoke rather boldly, looking at Eleanor directly, her hands balled into defensive little fists.

"Eaten by dogs," Eleanor said weakly. "What nonsense have they been telling you? Of course not. Come through into the kitchen."

Anne Thwaite turned away from the range where she was rattling up the fire into a fury and stood with hands on hips, poker in hand and stared from the child to Eleanor. "What a brazen nerve the woman has. Talking about kin. The girl has a father. A grandmother. What are you? A cousin, what, twice, thrice removed. And only by rumour."

"It's true. My blood is from the Denvers."

"Even so."

Jayne regarded the poker. "Are you going to put me in the fire?"

Anne looked at the waif for a moment or two as if she knew not to cry nor shout, then decided on a laugh. "Put you in the fire? Why girl, there's not a scrap of flesh on those bones. A dreadful roast you'd make." She put the poker down on the table. "I can tell by the look of you that you're riddled with dirt and lice.

I'm heating up a good pot of water, and then I'll be putting you in the bath."

Jayne pulled a face.

Eleanor put her hands together. She'd gotten through worse trials than this. So much for her assumption that she could relax in her dotage. It was decided that quickly and simply, without discussion or words spoken. Jayne would be staying. She looked briefly at the girl's clothes, worn so thin, with holes in places. They were not worth saving. "When she's in the bath, just put her clothes on the fire."

Anne nodded. "They'll be riddled. We'll hear the popping of bugs, no doubt."

"I'll go upstairs. I still have a few of Muriel's clothes from when she was a girl. They'll do until we can some new clothes made up."

A tiny nugget of hope appeared on Jayne's face. "I'm to have a new dress?"

"Perhaps you will," Anne said. "But don't you be taking anything for granted."

Months before Jayne Heaton was ceremoniously dumped on Eleanor, and around the time that Temperance's baby was failing, Kaarel Must was in Edinburgh worrying about dried peas. How old were best? For if they were too desiccated and ancient, it seemed as though no amount of water would swell them. But if they were too fresh, the swelling would not be enough to take any effect.

Kaarel dipped his hand into the little sack of dried peas and for a moment forgot he was in the underbelly of the hospital. He savoured that moment of the dry, hardened little bodies rolling against his chapped, chemical-stained hands. The peas willingly parted for his fingers. He let out a sigh and glanced up just as a rat scuttled across the far corner of the room. Was it jealous of the peas, or would it still prefer to gnaw on offal and corpses whenever it could?

"I always said this was a dirty source of knowledge."

Kaarel took his hand out of the peas, guiltily, and looked around. "Why, Dr Erskine MacKenzie," he greeted his old fellow student. "You are back from the Highlands?"

"For a few weeks. On business to Edinburgh. And to visit old friends."

"I am very pleased to see you." Kaarel hurried forward, extending a hand in greeting. They looked at the stained palm and Erskine kept his hands in his pockets. He'd done his time in the dissecting rooms, learning the human body and his trade. As a doctor it was inevitable he had to deal with corpses. But he had never been comfortable down in the mortuaries, where the corpses came and the dissections occurred. Where bones and body parts were cut and preserved for further research and learning, and if truth be told, for the sheer gruesome delight of some very odd collectors.

He nodded to the bag of peas. "I hope you're not preparing your supper down here."

Kaarel laughed. "I find I don't have much of an appetite when I'm at work. These are recommended by Mr Pole. You put them in dried, add water and they expand gently, slowly. It's a good method for separating the bones of the skull without causing too much damage."

The head, only freshly sawn, was looking away from them as if unable to contemplate what was about to be committed.

"So it's true, you've given up medicine?"

"Hardly, my good man. I'm at the head of it, so to speak. I've more orders in than I can keep up with. Samples and preserved dissections, and more requests for craniums than we get the heads for. We've been experimenting with alum water to get the right bone-white people want on their skulls."

Butchery, Erskine thought. "You had such a steady hand, and such a way with patients. We always said you'd be an excellent surgeon."

Kaarel lowered his eyes. "I find I work best in silence."

"One just has to learn to turn a deaf ear to the screaming. And it is over very quickly. The improvements to people's day to day lives..."

"We were not all born to be brilliant surgeons. And I am bringing great improvement to people's lives. Research and study is the way forward. This will bring about a better understanding of how the human body works."

"You're not getting in with that phrenology crowd are you?"

Kaarel grinned. "You've been up in the sticks too long. It's all anyone talks about, and all the collectors are looking for good quality, well-cleaned skulls. Edinburgh's just got its own Phreneological Society. We're meeting tonight; you should come."

"Away, man," Erskine groaned. "You've not actually joined in with such nonsense?"

"There are some great minds there."

"Don't you mean skulls?"

"That as well, but the skull shows what is underneath. Surely you've read Gall's work?" Kaarel went over to the basin to clean his hands. "He's done a lot of work on the brain itself. It's fascinating. I have completed my own dissections, following his instructions and studies, and seen what he has written about. It's not all balled up in the centre. The nerves flow outwards. You cut a brain apart the right way and you can see this. Nerves spanning right out to the outer reaches. It makes sense then that the skull, the very outer casing…"

"I'd rather talk about this in other settings," Erskine interrupted. "Get that butcher's uniform off you and let's get out into the air."

Kaarel broke into a boyish grin, took the hint and stopped talking. He quickly cleaned himself, took off his aprons, and fetched his coat. Collecting his bag, he made certain his bible, Thomas Pole's *Anatomical Instructor*, was there, and strode out of the dissection room with Dr Erskine MacKenzie.

That evening there was a meeting of the Edinburgh Phrenological Society, as founded by the Combe brothers, which Kaarel Must eagerly attended. He persuaded Erskine to accompany him as a guest. Erskine reminded himself that Must needed to be in with these people, for if he was producing fine specimens, they would be a great source of custom for him. Phrenology was all the rage, and whilst everyone in the know owned one of those glazed pottery heads with all the markings of the skull, what any self respecting student needed, like air, was an actual skull. And once they had one human skull in their possession, a collection was a necessity, for without others to compare with, a single skull was meaningless.

Erskine understood the importance of dissection and research; he was not denying this basic fact. The men who had the steady hand and stomach for it were an important part of their medical trade. But he remained unconvinced that by feeling lumps and indentations in the skull, by taking measurements, one could work out a person's personality and worth. He simply could not believe that a man's very essence was marked by the shape of his bones.

He sat and politely listened to the lectures and conversations that went on in-between during the meeting. George Combe, a wild-haired man with a rather large domed forehead (or was that due to a receding hair line?) and one of the founding members spoke in a voice of authority and stared down with contempt anyone who even questioned an aspect of his theories. Combe had spent a great deal of time thinking on these matters and what he knew were facts as far as he was concerned. He was, although not wishing to labour the point, the country's leading authority on phrenology. There were rumours circulating that he was going to write a book and it was going to be great. Erskine wondered how a lawyer was a better expert on the human body than the great men of medicine of Edinburgh, but he was merely a silent voice of cynicism awash in a broiling sea of adoration.

After the meeting a small number, thankfully not the Combes, went off to an inn for ale and pie for supper. Erskine was relieved that it was a group of medical men, and talk soon drifted off from phrenology and onto other matters. One man, who lectured at the university, was laughing about a woman who had come to visit him the other week. "She was asking me about studying at the university."

"For her son?"

"Lord, no! That's the madness. She thought she could come."

The punch line was followed by a serious of chortles and serious gruffling at such a preposterous notion.

"Why, women do not have the rational constitution for such an intellectual profession."

"They don't have the concentration or the brain capacity."

"They would be far too distressed at the sight of the sick."

"There are some female nurses..." someone dared to mention.

"Drunken prostitutes the lot of them. They've lost their female sensibilities and so can cope with the care of the sick."

"But they are only cleaning and watching. It requires an entirely different mental constitution to assess and diagnose. To plan the actual healing."

One of the men nudged Kaarel in the ribs. "And you certainly wouldn't want women in your place of work."

"Not unless they're corpses!" another laughed.

"Feinting all over the place. Why, women cannot stand the sight of blood."

Kaarel Must smiled weakly and finished the last of his ale. He would not commit any opinion to the light hearted discussion, but muttered something about fetching a top up and stood up from the table.

"That's the way, my man. Fetch another round in for us all."

When Kaarel returned with a jug of ale, they were toasting Erskine MacKenzie's impending marriage. One of the reasons for him coming to Edinburgh had been to purchase goods for the bride. Kaarel was a little surprised his friend had not mentioned it, although Erskine said that the mortuary had not felt an appropriate setting for such joyful announcements. Kaarel swiftly downed his drink and went back in search of further inebriation.

By the end of the evening Kaarel Must was so drunk he could barely walk. It was raining heavily when the group left the inn and dispersed to their individual lodgings. Kaarel stumbled down the street, tripped over a cobble and rolled over into a filthy puddle.

"By God, man," Erskine breathed as his heaved his sopping friend back onto his unsteady feet. "You're as drunk as a lord. I thought you Russians could take your drink. Here, put your arm around my neck."

"Estonian." Kaarel muttered.

"Yes, well, I'll bet they still take a wee nip in Estonia."

What was a five minute walk took fifteen. Everything blurred then split out into doubles within Kaarel's vision. He felt very heavy headed and did not particularly care to arrive anywhere. "You are lost to me now."

"I'm still here."

"You are to be married."

"Must, you're not one of these who says men of learning should not be married, for it distracts us?"

"No, indeed," Kaarel mumbled. "For you are in a position to have both." And with that he collapsed on the front door step of his lodgings.

"What did happen to you when you were away?" Erskine wondered to himself as he gritted his teeth and heaved his friend in through the doorway. No one had ever managed to get a satisfactory answer as to where Kaarel had gone when surgery had overwhelmed him. What had he been doing all those months, where had he lived? Or perhaps the even more pressing question: what had prompted him to return. They had spent countless hours together, and on some levels Erskine thought he knew him as well as his own mind, yet on other levels Kaarel was an utter enigma that made no sense.

There a fire glowing lowly in the room when the door was shoved open. Dropping the snoring Must into the shabby armchair, Erskine went to the fire and put a few more lumps of coal onto the fire. He shook back the bed covers then returned to his friend.

"You're soaked; you'll catch your death like this," he said as he removed Kaarel's shoes and socks. "I've known many a drunk go that way, and you're no experienced drunkard."

Next went the overcoat, jacket and waistcoat. The breeches were dropped and as he lumbered Must over to the bed, the shirt tails flopped up as the body was slung to the bed. Muriel woke up just as Erskine learned the truth about Kaarel Must.

"By God, man..." he uttered, the mismatched word coming out automatically.

"Oh no," Muriel wailed, tugging roughly at her shift to protect her modesty. "You mustn't know."

"You're..." Erskine couldn't quite grasp it all. Everything was an illusion. Or was he so drunk he couldn't trust his eyes?

"You mustn't tell. This is all I've ever wanted since I was a girl."

"To be a man?"

"To study."

Erskine ran a hand over his face and was surprised to find he was shaking. "Who are you?"

"I'm me," Muriel sighed drunkenly.

"But Kaarel Must?"

"It's just a name. I so wanted to study." Muriel started to cry. She had worked so hard. She had completed her studies at the university. She had paid employment. She was highly respected as a doctor. The other doctors spoke to her as an equal. She read all the latest papers. She was doing research. She had found her place. She felt alive. She looked up at Erskine whose face was grey. "Oh Erskine, my dearest friend," she sobbed. "Don't desert me now." She reached out for mercy and slipped off the edge of the bed. Erskine caught her and the two struggled to get her back on the bed. "You have been the greatest friend a man could have," Muriel continued. "You are my best friend. Oh, I do love you."

Erskine did not know what to do with himself when Muriel threw her arms about his neck. "Kaarel, I shouldn't.... don't you know... I can't call you Kaarel."

"You must, or else it is the end of my work."

All his fine work. Kaarel was a lie, a cover, a false identity. But the work was the same, regardless of the name. Those steady hands everyone had agreed would be excellent for surgery. A man that examined brain tissue during dissection. Penmanship who authored papers. This was all the work of a woman. Everyone said women were not up to any of this: the intensity of study, the knowledge, the steady hands, the calmness in face of blood and gore. Kaarel hadn't been able to cope with the screaming, but there were plenty of men who couldn't deafen their ears to it either.

"Who are you?"

"My name is Muriel MacCaskill," she told him. "And I must get out of this wet shirt."

The following day Dr Erskine MacKenzie cut his trip to Edinburgh short and started his journey back to his home of Plockton on the West Coast of Scotland. Kaarel Must continued with his work, albeit, with a sickly, longing air, for the next five or six months until he had to accept that nature was overtaking him and he needed to leave Edinburgh. He cited a dying mother, and travelled down to York, to be greeted by Elizabeth MacCaskill, who shrieked with a mixture of utter horror and joy when she learned that her little sister, who was supposed to be living as a man in order to pursue her dream life, was now with child.

Muriel stayed in relative secrecy with her sister for the rest of her confinement. Nolwenn, Elizabeth's ladies maid, shook her head and flung up her hands in despair. Never had she known two sisters who could make life far more complicated than it needed to be. They tried to persuade Muriel to contact the father; yes of course everyone in Edinburgh thought she was a man, but the father could not be so stupid. He wasn't married was he? Not when it happened, but he was now, she had heard. Well, who needed such a worthless man then? He was a good man, the best of friends. Best friends do not abandon each other like this. He does not know he has abandoned me, because he does not know of my situation.

Muriel fell into a depression over the winter. She did not wish to speak of babies or acknowledge the pregnancy despite the swiftly expanding belly set in front of her. She could only mourn what she had lost. Elizabeth tentatively suggested she might go back to her mother, for she could not stand in judgement given their parents had never really been married. All the children had been born out of wedlock. Muriel had no wish to communicate with anyone, and the more Elizabeth thought about the baby the less she pushed Muriel to reach out.

Elizabeth had thought that she was happy with her lot and the fact that she would never have children. They were a burden, far too much work, and a hindrance to indulgence and fun. But when it was certain Muriel would be with them for the duration, she became rather excited. She shopped for all the clothes, shawls and blankets in readiness, found a good midwife who was also willing to attend her apartments, and put word out for wet nurses around the due date just in case. When her sponsor came across some of the baby clothes, there was a moment of panic and almost the end of their understanding until Elizabeth made it clear she was sheltering her sister for a short time. It was the sister who had found herself in the family way. Two days later, when he had returned to his official wife, Elizabeth had regarded herself in the mirror and put her hands to her waspish waist. What kind of idiot could think this body near giving birth?

Being a student and medical practitioner, Muriel both knew and had practical experience of birth. She had seen how much women suffered, and how incapacitated they could become. Yet she remained under the rather naive assumption she'd be able to deal with her own birthing, until the day she went into labour. For the first few hours she did manage on her own, assuring Elizabeth that as she understood what was happening with her body, it would not hurt and she could deal with it. Elizabeth didn't believe the facial expressions or grunts, and besides which, her sister was now the size of a barrel. No woman of that shape could curl up to gain access to the point of action at the critical moment. She sent Nolwenn out for the midwife and sat in the room with Muriel, nodding and not believing a word that came out of her sister's mouth.

Later in the night the pain grew worse, and aside from blatant lying, Muriel wasn't able to say anything when a contraction came on. The midwife arrived, got her preparations ready and checked Muriel over. Muriel assured the woman that she was a doctor, to which the woman patted her hand and said of course she was, but at times like these what a new mother-to-be really wanted was another woman who had brought all kinds of babies, in all kinds of positions into the world.

Midnight passed, and Elizabeth remained with her sister throughout. She surprised herself by what a strong stomach she had, but also realised that despite being thrilled about the baby, she was very relieved she would never have to go through this herself. Nolwenn, in her down-to-earth, nonchalant way, calmly sauntered through the apartments, fetching requested items, and not batting an eyelid at the screams or the bloodied sheets she was passed to take away.

Somewhere in the wee small hours of early spring, a baby girl was born. Muriel flopped back into the bed, exhausted and disinterested. The midwife claimed it had been a very straightforward birth with very little tearing. The mother ought to make a good recovery. The infant screamed for attention, and Aunt Elizabeth, beaming and desperate, was ready with her fine shawls and swaddling clothes. She bundled the little girl up and held the little quivering parcel close.

"Muriel, will you not feed your girl? She is beautiful."

Muriel, who had not even set eyes on her daughter, rolled over in bed and refused to speak to anyone.

The midwife gave Elizabeth a pointed look. "I know a lass who needs the money. Her own babe only died two days ago. There was something wrong with him when he was born. I only needed a glance to see his mind was not there. It was a pity he lasted those two months, for the mother got attached to him. I'll send for her if you like. She'll be glad of the money and the roof, and she's enough sense of life about her not to have issues with your situation, if you catch my meaning."

The wet nurse was arranged, and between her and Elizabeth, all the love and sustenance a babe could require was available. After a few days Muriel finally allowed Elizabeth to put her daughter in her arms. She could not bond with the girl, but managed to name her, giving a nod to her heritage by choosing a Gaelic name, Mairi. She could do no more, she said, and sat and cried for hours in her bedchamber, thinking of all her work waiting for her in Edinburgh and how it was true that a woman could not do it. Not because she was incapable, but because biology got in the way. A child took over everything. Nothing else could matter in a life.

Mairi sensed that her mother was not interested, Nolwenn was certain, and for the first week barely seemed to stop crying. Muriel sobbed in a different room, and would sometimes howl at night when the baby's cries became too much. In the second week things settled down, and Mairi was happy with the embraces of her wet nurse and Aunt Elizabeth.

"So," Nolwenn proclaimed as she brought fresh clothes to the nursery. "We have found our routine. She is happy."

Muriel loitered in the doorway like a shadow as this proclamation was made. The two women looked up at the sound of her footsteps. Mairi grunted in Elizabeth's arms and snuffled around. Muriel peered down uncertainly at the child. "Might I?"

The moment Mairi was passed to her mother's arms she started screaming. Muriel was so horrified she almost dropped the bundle, Elizabeth catching the little babe. Nolwenn put an arm around Muriel's thin shoulders and let her back to the bed chamber. "I know you have not slept this past week. You must rest to regain your strength."

That night was restful, and even Mairi took a good five hours through the darkest part of the night. In the early morning the wet nurse was up again to feed the child. Elizabeth rose a few hours later, hoping that her sister had managed to rest somewhat and might be up to holding her daughter. When she opened the door she found Nolwenn stripping the bed.

"What are you doing?"

Nolwenn straightened and looked petulant. "Cleaning. This room needs to be cleaned and aired."

"Where is Muriel?"

Nolwenn shrugged. "Gone. I don't know. But her clothes and books are gone." She paused, making a pointed stare. "All of the clothes."

"Muriel and Kaarel's clothes."

"Damn you, Muriel," Elizabeth muttered, storming back out of the room. Her sister could be anywhere, under any identity. And what of her daughter? All she had done was give her a name and walk out on her. As if she was the first women to ever have a child out of wedlock. The first to ever have her heart broken. She had thought Muriel had a stronger countenance, but clearly she was wrong. She walked through to the nursery. Little Mairi was awake and contented, watching the light flicker over the ceiling. Elizabeth leant forward and stroked the girl's soft little cheek. "Don't you worry," she cooed. "Your mamma is here now."

All girls need their mothers. Muriel was travelling back to Haworth. She'd tightened her stays to hold her sagging, bulbous stomach in and headed off for the post carriages in the night. She could not do what was expected of her. So she journeyed to Haworth, and after months of silence, suddenly appeared at her mother's doorstep. Things had changed, for there was a little girl playing in the parlour she did not know. The housekeeper called for Jayne to come to her. Perhaps this was one of Anne's granddaughters. Muriel offered her mother no explanation to any of the questions, and like a wasted ghost slumped up to her room and went to her bed where she slept solidly for the next three days. She went in and out of fever, much to Eleanor's concern. Eleanor and Anne Thwaite cleaned up Muriel, concerned to see how much she bled. Anne raised her eyebrows and tutted and made a comment that they both knew at what times in a woman's life she bled that much. The physical signs, to two women who had birthed children, were too obvious to have any other explanation, but Eleanor couldn't believe it. Muriel had always been so sensible and had never been an attraction to men. But she had no idea where Muriel had been or what she had been doing all this time. Muriel was here at home, but she felt lost to her.

The next week brought more news in letter. Emmerline had given birth again, this time to a son whom she had named Mowbray. Finally her husband was satisfied that she had completed her wifely duties. What was more shocking was the letter at the end of the week. Eleanor dropped it when she saw the name at the end, and had to grip the door frame for a moment, feeling her heart wildly racing.

"Are you quite all right?" Anne came to her side and walked her to an armchair.

"Yes, just a little shock winded me."

Maud, a bemused shadow, wandered in the corridor and picked up the abandoned letter. Her eyesight was not good these days and she had never been a particularly good reader even at her peak. She smiled at the paper as if it were a little lamb, then looked around for the shepherd.

"Ah, my child," she said, noting Eleanor and coming through. She didn't recognise many people these days and was often confusing the names Eleanor and Gillian to the point she had given up and simply referred to her daughter as child. It made Jayne giggle, for Eleanor was such an old woman and certainly no child.

Maud pottered in and absently passed Eleanor the letter. Anne went back to the baking, listening to Jayne's childish screams of joy as she played outside. Maud fell asleep by the fire. Eleanor read the letter through twice before leaning back in the chair, meditating on what she had learned, before she read it a third time. Then she cried for lost years and wondered if she had done more or tried harder all that time ago, everyone's lives could have worked out better. Folding up the letter she walked upstairs and entered Muriel's room.

Muriel sat by the window and stared vacantly outside. She didn't react when her mother appeared. Eleanor coughed and walked into the room, sitting down on the end of the bed.

"I have had a letter from Elizabeth."

No reaction.

"Your sister."

Muriel felt sick. She did not dare look at her mother.

"I have not heard from her since I last saw her in Scarborough. It has been many years. In fact, sometimes I have wondered if she was still alive. She says she is very well. I just wish..." she left that last thought hanging in the room. What good would it do now? "You have been seeing her?"

Muriel looked across at her. Her face was blotched, a mixture of fear and embarrassment.

"I'm not angry with you. We all knew that things were left difficult between she and I. But she is asking if I have seen you. You must have been seeing her. She is worried." What has been happening to you? Eleanor wanted to cry out. Has my eldest drawn you into her world of debauchery and courtesans?

"I can write and tell her you are here of course..."

Muriel nodded meekly.

"She has news as well. She has recently had a baby. Mairi."

Muriel stared out of the window.

"She does not mention if she is married, but I assume she is still kept..." Eleanor waved the letter a little hopelessly in the air then set it on her lap.

Muriel nodded and bit her bottom lip. It was for the best. She could not care for a child. It would be better for Mairi to grow up with Elizabeth. She would not contest the lie.

"May I send your congratulations?"

"You may."

She stared at the side of her daughter's pale face. Perhaps she was putting the clues together and creating an incorrect storyline for her two daughters. But Muriel would not communicate with her. She was going along with this letter, whether it spoke the truth or not. "So I suppose this makes me a grandmother, although I doubt if I shall ever meet this girl."

She stood up. Laughter drifted up from outside.

Muriel's brow creased. "Who is that girl?"

"Who? Jayne? She is Temperance's eldest."

"Temperance?" Muriel sounded confused. Yes, she remembered the girl getting married a few years ago. Her father went through a phase of stalking their house. Like a wild, rabid dog of the moors, he loitered out there in the darkness. "But why..."

"She hung herself last year." Eleanor spoke harshly, glad to see the revelation shocked Muriel and made her turn fully in the seat to face her mother. "Of course we lied and said she died of grief in her bed so she might be buried. Her youngest died when he was just a babe."

"And we have Jayne."

"She is a distant cousin, as it transpires." Eleanor shrugged. "So she stays here. It seems I am a collector of problems."

Matters were made official later in the day when they had another visitor to the house. An officious little man Eleanor vaguely recognised, who carried a board with papers attached. He had come to the door as Eleanor had been passing, and looked a little surprised when she herself answered.

"I thought you had staff."

"Excuse me?"

He waved a pencil at her as if that ought to explain it. "I'm making the count, you know, every ten decades. I know the area quite well so I am managing a lot of the houses myself."

"The census," Eleanor breathed. It was only the third time it had been taken in the country, and a mere irritant to most, but she had an odd relationship with it. When the first one had been taken in 1801 she had been living over in Whitby. The local priests were supposed to conduct the surveys, but she had been pressurised into doing the work on that occasion. She knew about the census better than most. "You have to ask people. You can't assume you know."

"Bit simplified this year. They only want numbers and ages. No names. Your house is a bit of an uncertainty for me. Your daughter isn't always in residence, and I've heard you've taken in a ward."

"Yes, there's four of us; myself, my mother, my daughter, and little Jayne. I suppose you could call her a ward."

"I thought you had a housekeeper."

"She doesn't live in."

"Ah, that would explain it. Four females then. That'll do it." He scribbled something down on his papers, before looking up at her, almost surprised that she was still there. "Much obliged to you, Mrs MacCaskill. I'll be on my way; lots more people to count."

Eleanor stepped into the garden to watch him trot away down the lane. What a perfect job for nosey gossips. One day, every ten years to have complete justification to go about asking questions of every household. And now Jayne was officially a part of the MacCaskills. One of the four females. Another life Eleanor was responsible for.

It had been a long hot summer. People's demands on her felt relentless and without end. Maud barely recognised anyone these days. She was unaware of the year. Both Eleanor and Anne Thwaite reminded her every morning that it was the year of 1824, but by luncheon she had forgotten and was under the impression she was a maid of seventeen and not an elderly lady of 79 years. Sometimes she forgot that it was night during the midnight hour, and would attempt to leave the house to go to who knew where. Nights were disruptive, sleep was scattered and days became dull and muted. Eleanor was certain the effect was worse than with a newborn. She hired a night maid to help with the constant supervision. The new maid was an older woman who had fallen on hard times when her husband had drunk away the family farm before absolving himself of the consequences by dying. The woman had been left with nothing and was glad of the work.

After several happy months, the very presence of Jayne Heaton had started to distress Maud, and in turn this upset Jayne. There had been no aggravation or arguing, and Jayne had always been very respectful towards the older lady. Yet relations had disintegrated, and with a woman whose mind was lost, there was no negotiation or discussion possible. The two couldn't live together, yet Eleanor felt obliged not to abandon either. She'd heard from neither Jayne's grandmother nor father since the girl had been dumped on her doorstep like a sack of unwanted clothes. The girl needed an education. When Eleanor's own children had been growing up, she had hired tutors, but this wouldn't work in their disintegrating household.

She'd found her answer by suggestion from the local reverend, who mentioned a boarding school he was intending to send his own two eldest daughters to. Eleanor was grateful for the advice.

She still shunned the church, which made conversation a little terse with the man at times. In fairness, Bronte did not go about preaching and attempting to convert the more eccentric when he was not at his regular work. Beyond his profession, it was known that he preferred his own company in his study to being out among the parishioners. Whatever he had done, people would have complained, for there was nothing like feeling put out and disadvantaged due to some imaginary slight from a vague figure in one's life. And so people grumbled about foreigners when the subject of religion came up, and particularly the Irish as if they did not know how to behave in society. It was unjust, Eleanor thought, for the man had six children to raise. His wife had been dead three years already. His sister-in-law lived with the family and was an asset, but even so, he had a lot to contend with. She did not always agree with his opinions, but on the whole Eleanor felt his to be a liberated and reasonable mind. When he suggested Cowan Bridge, she wrote to school mistress to arrange Jayne's education.

Muriel was back at home. After a few months lingering shadow-like following the birth of Elizabeth's daughter, she had packed her things and disappeared once again for almost a year. Eleanor was discarded without a thought or a word, and would have been again without contact with any of her children, were it not for the start of an awkward and slow correspondence with her eldest daughter, Elizabeth. The two had yet to meet, despite the relatively short distance between, and Eleanor had not seen Mairi, but it was a start. Mairi would be three now, and she wondered what kind of an upbringing the girl would experience, living with a kept woman. Perhaps she'd see her father a little less that her own children had seen Angus, for he had been absent for long periods every year when the droving road called to him. Perhaps all the worry and judgement came more from preconceptions rather than fact, but it was difficult to keep a disapproving tone out of her letters when she remained at such a distance, even now after three years only permitted to read descriptions of Mairi.

About a year after her disappearance Muriel started to return to Haworth. That is to say the crates began to arrive, marked with the name Kaarel Must, care of Muriel MacCaskill. Muriel's room was full to the rafters. When she herself appeared in person, she declared there was no space to work and commandeered the attic. She spent weeks clearing out and preparing the work space before she began shifting furniture and the precious contents of her cases up into her sanctuary. There was no explanation offered as to where she had been, or what her plans were now, but a great many letters came for this stranger, Dr Must, and Muriel was constantly writing at her desk. Not just letters to send out, although there were a great many replies sent, but from what Eleanor could ascertain, there was a book being written. She had been up into the attic a few times, and had been a little surprised by what she found. Muriel had always enjoyed scientific books, some illustrated, but to discover bones and jarred preserved samples of human body parts was more than a little disconcerting. She tried to talk to Muriel as to what she was doing, but Muriel's face closed on her, then Maud started shouting at someone who was not in the room, Jayne began to cry because she thought she had done something wrong, and Eleanor felt like giving up on the lot of them and taking to the road again. And so the months went by and turned into years, and she gave up trying to work out Muriel's life. At least she knew where her daughter was geographically, and that was some level of reassurance. She had to take what she could get.

The year had just turned to September. There was peace in the house. Maud was sleeping, Anne was ordering her kitchen and the night maid had gone out shopping. Muriel had left an hour or so ago on some vague mission to attend to a boy who had been sick these past two weeks and was leaving the local doctor confounded. Eleanor wasn't exactly sure what Muriel thought she was going to do, but she had informed her mother she was off to Pondens for the day, and quite frankly, to see Muriel out of the house and in daylight was a blessing in itself. Eleanor sat in her garden and regarded the trees. The summer had been long and dry and the leaves were already turning. Here begins our autumn, she thought, and ran a hand over her face. The skin on her hands felt thinner, and she could feel creases and wrinkles on her face, reminders that she was no longer the young woman who still resided in her mind and her soul. When did I grow so old, Eleanor wondered. Now I am past sixty. I am the only one of my siblings left. Will I go on to become my own mother, forgetful and confused, talking to shadows rather then real people?

Chatter from a nearby track distracted her from contemplation and she watched as the Garrs sisters, who worked at the parsonage, went out walking with the four youngest Bronte children. Three girls and a boy. They were an odd little crew who did not connect much, if at all with the other village children. The boy walked at the head of the pack, pushed on by the servants into position of leader. There was a lot of expectation put on him, being the only male child of a father who had excelled in his profession and studies. What if he did not live up to expectation?

The little girl, Emily, only about six years of age, looked over her shoulder rather suddenly as if Eleanor's musings had been screamed out loud. A pretty slight creature who was not settled in herself. Her stare was demanding and confrontational, whilst at the same time almost terrified of itself. She met Eleanor's eye, even from this distance and held it until she tripped over a pebble, and had to turn her attention back to walk.

Eleanor picked up her shawl from the grass where it had fallen and stood up. She had nothing to do, and everyone else was out walking, enjoying the sunshine. Why not? She left the garden and headed down to the track. Perhaps she could go and see what Muriel was doing, try to show an interest in her daughter from a different point of attack and see if Muriel would open up to her. She walked downhill towards the village of Stanbury, then along to the hamlet of Ponden, but thought better of intruding as she approached the scattering of buildings. Instead she followed a track past corn fields, a mill pond, then onwards to a deep glen, that carried a rivelet down from the high moors. Despite the sharp incline, Eleanor increased her pace and walked swiftly up the old dusty track. She savoured the heightened pump of blood and the intensity of breathing. She felt her spirit soar and remembered her childhood on the moors of Commondale, miles and miles from here, out playing in the wilderness with her girlhood friend, Atheleys, then running errands and taking post from village and farm to the next with her little donkey. If she closed her eyes it could almost be yesterday, and yet simultaneously a chapter from a book she once read and nothing more. Where had all those decades gone?

As she rose in altitude and left the glen for the open moor, the skirts of her dress swept through the heather, crackling at the dry, hardened stems and knocking bursts of heather scent up into the air. The flowers still bloomed purple and the colour sang against the horizon. Her shawl was caught in the crooks of her arms, and hung loosely down her back. Her hair, thick with white strands these days, standing out against the dark, was roughly knotted up on her head, with a cloth scarf tied around her head rather than a bonnet for some sake of decency. Eleanor had never been one to attend too closely to fashion. She turned to gaze back down the valley towards the lower lands and the hamlets and farms.

In her periphery she saw a young man in a long coat striding through the heather with ease. The angle of the sun caught in her eye and she could not make him out. She felt a hand to the small of her back and a warm voice close to her ear. "Come with me."

Eleanor lowered her eyes and smiled sadly. She shook her head. "I'm not ready just yet."

"Just a while longer, eh?"

She looked up and the young drover smiled at her. The Scots in his voice was impossible not to recognise. He was in his thirties, in his prime, the young man he once was. The long coat flapped around his legs and they look up to the sky where clouds were gathering, copper highlights brushed around the edges, but an overall gloomy countenance. There was a storm coming, much needed rain, but after a drought too much at once could cause trouble. Eleanor looked to her feet, to the dried out peat which felt springy and crust-like when walked upon. It had been sun baked and desiccated over the summer and was not ready for a deluge.

"Come away with me."

"Angus, I..."

He smiled and offered his arm. The rain started to patter around them. "I don't think it would be wise to stay just here on the hill. Perhaps we'll walk over to the ridge across there."

I followed you up and down this country when you were alive, Eleanor thought as she accepted the arm and walked out with this ghost. They left Crow Hill and trod through the heather, aiming for a higher ridge. The rain became torrential and the drover took off his long coat, neatly swung it around and sheltered

Eleanor. The collar was up on top of her head so as to provide a waterproofed cave for her to stay dry in. She looked at him as if to protest that he needed the coat as much as she, but he merely smiled. "The rain doesn't bother me none, these days."

They continued to walk until they reached the high ridge, then stopped side by side and looked back the way they had come. The hill already looked a distance through the rain, and the lower levels with buildings a hazy sketch not easy to distinguish from the pouring water.

"This much water so suddenly after a hot dry period is not good. It unsettles the earth," Eleanor said as she stepped up against the drover. "I remember when I was growing up, on the moors, there'd sometimes be trouble."

"Aye, that there will," he muttered.

The thunder clapped again. The electric immensity of the heavens rumbled out across the landscape as if it were a mere patchwork and toys. The atmosphere felt to be pulsating. Another rumble started, not of the heavens but of the earth, and the very ground they stood upon shook. Eleanor's eyes widened and she looked around to Angus, gripping his arm. She'd seen the odd little bog burst in her childhood, but this felt as though the very earth was about to crumble.

She could not quite believe what happened. The hill where they had first met started to melt. With the deluge of rain it became a churning body of water and dark peaty earth, shifting and moving. The dried out husks of earth hadn't been able to soak up the torrential rain quickly enough. The water had poured through until it hit the layer of shale. There was nowhere to go and so the whole mass started to bubble and move. It picked up momentum, then an area perhaps half a mile across began to move downwards as if alive. A rolling body of watery earth, losing control as gravity took over. It slunk over the edge and rushed into the steep glen which Eleanor had recently ascended.

Eleanor gasped and staggered forward a few metres. That sludge train would be heading straight down towards Ponden. What could she do? She stopped, realising she wouldn't be able to go back the way she had come. "Oh Lord," she wailed, terrified of what may happen to Muriel, and being unable to warn her. She let the drover's coat slip down to her shoulders and felt the rain plaster her hair against her scalp. She turned, heather pulling at her skirts, to look to Angus for advice, but he had already gone. She was alone on the ridge. Her hands went to the collar of the old coat she had kept all of these years and pulled it about her body. She would have to trek around Crow Hill, giving it a very wide berth, and descend to the lower land further on, before backtracking along to Ponden. She just hoped Muriel was inside when it happened.

In fact Muriel had stepped out for air, insensible to the pouring rain, when the peaty black body started to roll down the glen. She stood and stretched her back, hands on hips, then lingered to watch some children playing in the lane. She wondered what Mairi was doing. The girl was three years old now and quite convinced that Elizabeth was her mother. Muriel visited now and then and worried that she ought not to be more upset that Mairi was Elizabeth's daughter and not her own. Kaarel told her it was nothing to worry about. Everyone was different and Mairi was in good hands, surprisingly considering how Elizabeth supported herself. Muriel wouldn't have known what to do with a baby and would have been miserable. It would have been the end of her life. She wouldn't have been able to go back to Edinburgh to tie up her work so that Kaarel could relocate. Nor work on that final project of dissections and studies before she had returned to Haworth. The call for cadavers was immense; they had even been shipping them in from as far as West Yorkshire, bodies from accidents in the mills, people from the poor house who had expired and nobody wanted to bury. The money was always better than the last rites for a deceased. Then there were the more suspect bodies coming in. There were men who worked in Edinburgh collecting available bodies, bodies supposedly meeting the legal requirements for dissection, but they were a shifty sort who did not always meet one's eyes. A lot of the dissection men learned not to ask too many questions, and Muriel wondered if some were complicit. She recalled bumping into a man called Burke late one night and thinking there was something very amiss. Now was the time to return to Yorkshire and write Kaarel's masterpiece on the functioning of the human body.

Two of the little boys laughed as the girl tripped over and fell into a puddle. She started crying. It didn't really matter, for with all the rain, they were already soaking. Why did their mother not send for them? Muriel's gaze drifted, passing over the hills beyond as a mere backdrop, then her brow creased and she looked back, realising something was wrong. There was something filling up and coming down the glen. Dark, churning, and accompanied by the sound of thunder, or was it making the sound itself?

"Children!" she shouted, darting forward and dragging the girl out of the puddle. "We have to get inside now."

"What?" One of the boys stopped his play and stared gormlessly at her.

Muriel wasn't lingering to explain. She grabbed the boy by the arm, and with the little girl under her arm like a sack of flour, she ran back for the building, accompanied by children's shrieks and pattering footsteps. The very earth they ran along had started to rumble.

It took Eleanor some time to work her way safely around the gaping, sloppy crater on the moors and get to lower ground. As she headed back towards Ponden she was shocked by what she saw. The drama was over and the earth no longer moved, but the damage was unimaginable. The golden fields of corn were now covered in a sloppy, dark peaty mess and the mill pond had simply vanished. It must be several feet deep, she thought as she hurried around the edges, wondering exactly where Muriel might have gone. She bumped into the Reverend Patrick Bronte, who had hurried down from Haworth having heard the noise and reports that something had happened at Ponden – for nothing travelled as quickly as bad news.

"My children were walking this way. There has been an almighty earthquake."

"It was a bog burst. I saw it."

He shook his head, not really listening to her. "A terrible earthquake."

They found a slightly raised path and followed it. Shortly the Garrs sisters and the four youngest Bronte children came in to view, chattering about the drama, full of bravado now the danger was over. They had sheltered in a porch and had been very brave, although looking at their faces, it was clear that a few tears had been shed at the time.

Eleanor left them and continued towards Ponden. She felt her chest physically relax when she caught sight of Muriel, the bottom of her skirts filthy black, but well and talking to other locals. She paused mid sentence when she caught sight of her mother tramping through the refuse towards her. Wet hair was streaked over her face, her head scarf barely hanging on. That and the lengthy drovers' coat she insisted on wearing made her look barely respectable. Muriel touched the forearm of the woman she was talking to, then hurried forward to meet Eleanor.

"I don't know if there's been an earthquake or something. There was the thunderstorm and suddenly a sea of earth came down the glen," she chattered, waving her hand vaguely back in the direction of the hills. "Just a black wall racing down to us. I got the children inside. I don't think anyone has been hurt. I don't know what's happened."

Eleanor grasped her daughter's hands then pulled her forward and embraced her. "Thank goodness you're all right."

"I don't know what just happened." It was surreal, incomprehensible that earlier in the day there had been fields of corn, clean grassy tracks, even a pond, and now it had all vanished. All about lay nothing but black sodden peat.

"It was a bog burst. I saw it, I was up on the hills. On the ridge and I saw Crow Hill collapse."

"You were roaming about the moors in this weather?"

"It was sunny when I went out."

"Mamma, you are not young anymore…"

Eleanor rolled her eyes in exasperation. "I have walked the length and breadth of this country. I grew up on moorland. I can look after myself."

"You're not a young woman anymore."

"Muriel. Just stop this." Eleanor hugged her daughter again and watched the villagers pick their way through the peat sludge, greeting one another in a daze. "Are you finished here? Might we go home?"

"Yes," Muriel sighed. "We shall go home. You look a state."

Eleanor glanced down at Muriel's skirts, raising her eyebrows. "You're not that neat yourself at the moment."

"I did just survive an earthquake."

"Bog burst, I'll have you know." Eleanor corrected her. "I've never seen one so bad. Come along now, let's get home."

There was a new thing they called the railway. Many people, although admittedly not all, were very excited for the future. Two northern towns, Darlington and Stockton were now connected by lines of iron, and soon the rest of the country would be riding here and there in steam powered carriages following predestined iron tracks. More people could be transported at once, rather than being restricted to the confines of packed post carriages, or the gut-wrenching up and down of sea travel, and of course, everything was better than walking. The time of the drovers was up.

Muriel laid aside the newspaper and gazed out of the window. The autumnal world was soaked after heavy rains had beset the West of Yorkshire the last few days. It felt like a joke now that the clouds had rumbled away and the sun was once again permitted to touch the earth. Her mother was taking some respite from the intensity of the house by standing in the garden and neurotically twisting the ends of her shawl. It wouldn't help, but what more could Muriel tell her? She had tried to explain, but Eleanor had given her a strange look as if she had forgotten her place in the world and reminded her that she was not a doctor.

And she is right, Muriel thought. Muriel MacCaskill is not a doctor. And Kaarel Must does not exist. I am both and I am neither and I do not know where I reside. Kaarel had been back in Edinburgh for a couple of months earlier in the year. He had been well-received, particularly at the lodging house next door to where he rented rooms. There had been a great number of medical students who had studied part of his works on the human body, and were keen to praise it and ask tricky questions in equal measure, hoping to trip up the well-known anatomist. There were other young students in the house who had loitered at the side lines and watched. A young man with a large head and an air of obstinacy about him had stood and stared at Kaarel in a way that also said he knew. He knew that Kaarel was actually a woman. A woman who had abandoned her child. Don't worry about Simpson, the other students said as the strange young man wandered off. Studying art or some such thing, but fancies himself reading medicine instead.

The adoration of students was one thing, but standing within the medical community of Edinburgh was another, and Kaarel's frequent and long absences had taken their toll. He was not sure if he cared. It was all very well debating and spending evenings discussing theoretical matters or sharing horror stories of recent operations gone wrong, but what Kaarel wanted was to make a difference. The book, a hefty tome of human anatomy, was aiding students, but it was incomplete. There was, quite simply, so much they did not know, and until it was known, many diseases and maladies would remain untreatable. So many people struggled through the day to day due to a myriad of conditions. If only all these great minds could be focused on research, some practical benefit could be found. But energies were focused on sciences that increasingly looked like a waste of time. The Phrenology Society grew from strength to strength and yet what did they do? What was achieved? They sold a lot of specimens and measured heads, but really, they did not diagnose or cure anything. And Kaarel was less and less convinced that the shape of a head had any impact other than to control how a person looked. There had to be more to it to explain how a person's conscious thought functioned, and even more pressing, how and why it started to malfunction and continued to deteriorate.

This year had been a living case study, for her grandmother had rapidly fallen apart. She had reached the grand old age of eighty, but what was the point of it, if this was the state a body was to be in. She was skeletal and could no longer remember anyone's name, not even her only living daughter, Eleanor. She had conversations with people who were not there, and had to sleep in the downstairs parlour for she was convinced there was a gaping crevice upstairs. The woman her mother had hired to mind her and her night wanderings had grown bored and low and taken to gin. They'd had to let her go, much to most people's distress, but one invalid was enough, without having a second the family were actually paying to be on the premises. Thankfully they managed without the maid. Maud slept a great deal these days and did not have the strength to walk far. But she still had her moments, such as last night.

They had not realised she was gone from the house until the early morning. At which point Maud could have been outside for anything from half an hour to six or more hours. She was as soaked as a person could be, cold as death and not breathing well. Eleanor had found her rain-splattered into the earth just beyond their garden wall. She'd peeled her grubby mother out of the sloppy dirt and brought her inside. Muriel had helped to clean her up, and in fresh clothes, they'd gotten her into bed close by the fire. Her breathing was sparse and hoarse and she was not conscious, even when they had brought her into the house. She would not live long now. Muriel did not say so. Deep down her mother would know. Had Muriel said something, she would only be scolded that she was being maudlin. No one understood that she had a professional opinion more worthy than all the hacks living and working in the district.

Outside, little Jayne Heaton trotted out to Eleanor with a cup of something hot and steaming. There was another burden her mother did not need. Jayne had returned in the summer. Jayne had never thought ill of the boarding school where she had been sent, but then given where she had started life and how she had been abandoned by her family, her expectations were not particularly high. It didn't say much for the school that two of the Bronte children had caught some malaise and returned to Haworth in the late spring to die. Another family beset by tragedy. Well, they all were, Muriel thought. What family did not have a list of deceased, taken before their time? And so often but for common sense, they could have lived. She saw the filth some families lived in and it was a wonder any of them were still alive. Here in the lower streets of Haworth they drank the water that ran through the graves. One would have hoped that in paying fees and sending a child to an establishment supposedly aimed at bettering the child, they would at least remain alive. From increasing accounts, the children at that school, Cowan Bridge, had been kept abominably, living in freezing conditions and given little to eat, all because a child should learn its godly place and accept what it received and be grateful.

She sighed and leant back into the chair. But what was the point of leading a long life if one was to end up like her grandmother?

Muriel stood up and made her way downstairs. Eleanor was coming back into the house. Anne Thwaite had just left to fetch some items from the grocers, and had taken Jayne with her so that the girl might get some air. Eleanor looked as though she had aged years in the last few hours.

"Anne said she'll see if she can get some children at the top end to play with Jayne. She needs to run about but my mother needs the peace to rest just now. I'll just go check on her."

She was gone into the room only a moment or two before her voice rose in volume and tempo, a ringing of panic that wanted reassurance to the lies she was telling herself. "She sleeps so soundly and deeply I cannot hear her breath."

It is a mercy, if it is so, Muriel thought, heading for the parlour. Her grandmother, like a bleached, pared down little doll full of furrows and wrinkles of worry, pure white hair and not an ounce of fat on her, lay on her back, in fresh linens and at peace. The old wound on her upper jaw looked very pronounced today, but for the first time as though it caused her no trouble. It used to give Muriel nightmares as a child when she heard the stories of grandmother's girlhood toothache and the local blacksmith having a go. The tooth had stood fast but the man had managed to crack open her jaw and it had not healed up well. She ought well to have remembered that and realised she did not have the stomach for human suffering and pain.

"I should fetch the doctor," Eleanor chattered.

Muriel leaned over her grandmother. The old lady was no longer with them, it was only a corpse, but she went through the ritual of checking for signs, just to appease her mother. "She is dead, mamma." Muriel said. "I'm so sorry, but she has passed on."

"She is only sleeping. Oh Muriel, you are not a doctor. You don't know what you speak of." Tears were streaming down her mother's face.

"Shall I go and fetch the local doctor?"

"No, I shall go."

"I do not mind and you have had..."

"No!" Eleanor interrupted sharply. "I must get out of this house. You stay here and make sure little Jayne does not see her. She will be very upset. You will not mind staying with her. She is perfectly angelic compared to some of those things you keep in the attic."

Muriel sat in the chair beside the bed and listened to her mother leave the building. She looked at her dead grandmother, whose brain had died months ago, whose personality had gone long before that. She thought of her specimens upstairs. Of her tools and instruments. Of her research and her theories. She looked at her grandmother's head.

Eleanor returned with the doctor, Dr Bernard Hartlet, sooner than Muriel would have anticipated, had she recalled at all that the rest of the world continued. When she started her work, or rather when Kaarel Must began his work, everything else ceased to exist. Muriel sat at the side of the room and watched him work, fascinated by how much they had discovered already. Then she was up and at his side, aiding with the dissection. There was a loud creak as the warped door was opened. Muriel looked up sharply and Kaarel had disappeared.

The doctor, Dr Hartley who she vaguely remembered from somewhere, entered the parlour first. He stumbled over his complete shock, followed by horror, but to his honour regained his senses quickly and stopped Eleanor entering the room. "My dear lady," he almost roared, backing out and slamming the door. "You must not enter."

The door slammed and there were sounds of a struggle out in the corridor. Eleanor protested. Her mother and her daughter were in the room. Eventually there was some calming, and the sound of retreating footsteps. A man stood outside the door, gathering his thoughts and wondering how best to handle the situation. He set his bag on the floor and took out a glass and a small bottle.

Muriel's face brightened again as the doctor entered the room. A man of medicine would appreciate what she had done. "There's great holes," she said, gesturing to her work in progress.

"Great gaping holes. You can actually see the gaps in her memory."

"My dear Miss MacCaskill," the doctor started, stepping forward in a cautious manner as if approaching a wild horse that may bolt at any moment. "I think you have been working very hard and need to rest now."

"I can rest tomorrow," Muriel cast the thought aside, brandishing the bone saw and whipping it through the air as if it was a trivial thought. She did not look as though she meant to threaten, rather she had merely forgotten she was even holding the thing and was waving her hands about.

"We all know that sloppy work comes of tired hands," the doctor said. He held out the glass to her, his eyes on the wet saw. "I think it would be a good idea to drink this and rest a little."

"I suppose it would be prudent. And she won't be going anywhere." Muriel accepted the drink.

When the heavy dose of laudanum had taken effect and Muriel was asleep, the doctor carried her upstairs and deposited her in the first bed he found. He refused entry to all, and left Eleanor, her housekeeper Ann Thwaite, and her ward, Jayne Heaton, out in the garden whilst he methodically worked in the parlour. Ann Thwaite would be able to clean this up but none of them needed to see what had been done. He collected the dissected pieces and the top of the skull, fitting all together as best he could, before ripping up one of the bed sheets into strips to bind the head together. He used another sheet to mop up as much of the blood as he could, gathered up the instruments and bundled them into the sheet and carried it outside with the bag.

Three females stared at him in expectation.

"Mrs Thwaite," he started, noting the women's eyes go to the bloodied sheets he carried. He chose not to explain himself, instead placing the sheets, along with his bag on the ground as if they were all his private property. "Perhaps you could take the girl into the kitchen for her supper. Then reading in her room before bed."

"But what..."

"I'll need to..."

"Please!" He interrupted both women. "Miss MacCaskill is upstairs sleeping now. I think if you care for the child, then once she is in bed a little cleaning will be required in the parlour."

"Mrs Hurst has passed away then?"

He nodded gravely.

Anne and Jayne started for the door.

"Wait." He held up a hand. "If, or rather when you are preparing the body for burial... the washing and dressing... I have put some bandages about her head. It is of the upmost importance that you do not remove them."

Anne huffed and rolled her eyes. "Prepare a body without washing the face or brushing the hair?" She went to shove past him in a manner that suggested he was an idiot.

"Mrs Thwaite," he said sharply. "I must have your solemn promise on this matter, and yours, Mrs MacCaskill. It is of the upmost importance."

"But..."

"I insist."

Anne Thwaite shook her head at him. "Very well, if your handiwork is that precious. Come along Jayne, let's fetch a little something to eat."

Eleanor let out a sigh and sat down on the low stone wall of the garden. "Doctor Hartley, I do not understand why I am not permitted in my own house. Why you decided to bandage my mother's head? Why you have sent my daughter to bed?"

He walked across to her and handed her a small glass bottle. "This is laudanum. Your daughter is drugged. I would keep her so for the next few days until you can make arrangements for the best."

"For the best?"

"It is not my family, and I can only advise, but I would strongly suggest an asylum. I know a very good one in York."

"You must be joking."

"Admittedly I have never seen hysteria in the female take such a drastic turn."

"Dr Hartley. My mother has just passed away. This is a very difficult time, but I am not feeble minded and I do not like the riddles. Please speak plainly."

"I do not wish to shock a lady..."

"I am not some delicate fool. I have walked the length and breadth of this country. I have lived decades more and seen more than you can imagine. Tell me what you saw."

"I do not know how best to describe it," he laughed without humour, awkwardly looking about himself before gesturing to the wall as if he might take his place beside her. She nodded assent and he sat down. "And the strangest thing is, if I didn't know any better, didn't know what I had seen before me and the fact that your daughter must have done it, I would have said the work had been done by a skilled surgical hand. They were very fine specimens."

"Surgery? You're not trying to suggest my daughter tried to save my mother?"

"Oh no, your mother would have been quite dead, please do not worry on that account."

"So what is it?"

"Mutilation."

Eleanor stared at him as if he must be mad. Mutilation. Unnecessary chopping and cutting, removing and slicing. And then he had felt the need to bandage up Maud's head and impress upon them the importance that they do not remove the wrappings. What on earth had Muriel been thinking? Eleanor thought of the skulls and specimen jars that had come by the crate load from Edinburgh. The lines of heavy, learned tomes of science that adorned Muriel's living space. All the lost months and years living and doing who knew what and where. And now she had cut open her own grandmother's head. She closed her eyes. "Is nothing sacred?"

"Please do not blame yourself," he said, misunderstanding her body language. "This does sometimes happen with older spinsters who are still of an age... I mean, they are not so old that it would be impossible for them to have a child, but that they are now old for marriage. It's hysteria. Admittedly I have never heard of a case following such a pattern. But when a woman is taken from her calling..."

Eleanor kept her eyes closed so that she would not be tempted to slap the man. Hysteria. She'd occasionally heard mutterings of it before. As if women were less capable of dealing with life. What utter nonsense.

"She needs to be in an asylum. With proper care. Perhaps with time and the right treatment, she might be able to live again, quietly with family..."

"Keep her drugged up for the rest of her life?"

"No," the doctor smiled awkwardly. "She would build up a resistance. This is only good for the short term. But there are procedures that can be done. Not everyone must be locked away forever."

Generally, she believed the doctor to be a decent man. He would not be gossiping at the pub about what he found in Eleanor MacCaskill's parlour today. But word and rumour would get out. Oh Muriel, Eleanor inwardly wailed, what have you done? She would not be able to leave it a week and then let Muriel continue as normal. Everything would have to change. She let out a long draught of breath. "Would you allow me.... I would like to select the place and treatment for my daughter. You understand, I wish the best for her."

"I understand. Family ties are strong, regardless of what is committed. Permit me to write to you with some recommendations. Some names and addresses that at the very least could be a starting point for your enquiries."

"Yes, that would be very kind."

.

That would be very kind. The sentiment went round like an echo in Eleanor's head for the next couple of days. What was kindness? Where even was the point of it if this was where we were all to finish when all was done?

She kept her mother, bandaged up, in the coffin in the house for the two days before the funeral. Muriel remained drugged up on laudanum. She had wondered about leaving her daughter in a state of drug addled sleep until long after the funeral, but decided that it would be better to have her present in order to squash any potential rumours. In the evening the day before she missed a dose and Muriel began to come round. She was thick headed and looked dreadful, and needed to take her mother's arm to be led to the church, but that could all easily be blamed at the feet of grief. In the long hours lingering between death and funeral Eleanor had wondered why she did not break down, or attack her daughter for the crime she had committed against her very own grandmother. Instead she remained sharp and active. Perhaps it was shock that sustained her, and indeed the world about her felt a little other worldly, as if they were all only actors and none of this was real.

It did not seem that word had gotten out about Haworth regarding what Muriel had done. Although a brief word from the doctor made it clear that the truth would only be suppressed on condition that Muriel was taken away for treatment. Anne Thwaite, rather surprisingly, had managed neither to gossip about the event within town, nor to mention it in Eleanor's presence. Yet there was a sense of unspoken strain and Eleanor realised that Anne's time working for her would be nearing an end, as would Muriel's life in Haworth. And what of little Jayne Heaton, what was she to do with the girl? There was always the option of sending her back to her family, but as neither father nor grandmother had ever enquired after her nor sent any money or token for her upkeep, sending her away felt too much a cruelty to commit. She wondered about returning to Whitby, or even Commondale, but the years had moved on and both she and those places had changed. She did not know whether she could be comfortable in either again. But these were worries for later on, for now there was the question of what to do with Muriel.

The ceremony went by in a blur despite it being over the hour. There were another two funerals booked in for the day, so they could not linger, but even so, to Eleanor it felt as though it was all over before it had started. Maud was lowered into the ground, people paid their last respects, and as far as most were concerned, the chapter was now closed and finished. Forgotten. People came to her and muttered the usual lines, but she did not hear or notice most. A touch to the arm and she was surprised to see Emmerline before her.

"Emmerline, I… I thought your husband forbade you having anything to do with us."

She smiled sadly and shrugged. "He is not in charge of me," she said, not sounding convinced by her own statement. "Besides, she was my grandmother. I had to come and pay my respects. Are you... are you well?"

"I don't know what I am."

"And Muriel? She looks..."

Eleanor glanced across to her youngest, who loitered by the head of the grave, looking rather like an animated corpse. The world came rushing upon her as if a candle had been lit in the darkness. She was aware of the locals hovering. The appetite for gossip was as great as ever and ears were keen. "She's not been well." She looked to her niece. "I see you are expecting another happy event. Number four?"

She nodded shyly. "Yes, four more months to go."

"I hope it all goes well. Do try to send me news, a letter or something, when the baby is born. I would like to know. But only if it safe for you."

Emmerline looked a little confused but nodded her consent. Eleanor misconstrued the look, and assumed Emmerline had never come across the temper of men, the brutality, and how little worth they so frequently ascribed to women.

When the MacCaskill family returned from the funeral, all proceedings cleared and traditions upheld, Jayne was sent to bed early. Muriel, eyes bloodshot and skin with a sickly pallor, looked as though she would automatically trudge back up to her chamber, but Eleanor redirected her into the parlour. "You've kept out of it for two days, but now we must talk."

"Talk? Two days?" Muriel rubbed at her eyes. "I have never felt worse. And I have been in bed for two days? No wonder. What ails me?"

Eleanor stood in the doorway and looked on the woman in disgust. She meandered about before flopping into a chair as though all the pity lay upon her and life was troubling. Here sat the monster who had mutilated her mother's corpse. How could she be? Once she had been a sweet little child, so devoted to her books and always hovering about her mother. Eleanor had always known where she was. They had enjoyed a good relationship. Then Muriel had disappeared in all senses of the word and returned an impatient, impenetrable creature, and ultimately a heartless monster.

"Do you not remember what you did?"

Muriel squinted at her. "Did? When?"

"What you did to my mother." Eleanor hadn't realised she had a cup in her hand, but she threw it at the wall as she shouted. The smash and the roar brought Muriel out of her stupor, and she sat up a little straighter and actually looked a little frightened. "She was not but a minute dead in her bed, and you desecrated her."

What had she been doing before all of the lost time? Her memory was hazy. That her grandmother was dead she understood from the funeral, but then grandmother had been failing for months if not years so it had been expected. She looked down at her hands and felt the blood, now washed away. The scalpel in her hand, and before that the heavy work with the saw, the muscles in her arms pushing into the work as she cut neatly through the skull. That was what had happened. A perfect example of research, and some fantastic samples. One could actually see the deterioration in the brain, great holes where usually there ought to be brain matter. Whatever disease Maud had, it had been eating away at her brain from the inside out.

"My samples..." Muriel started as if to move out of the chair.

"Your samples?" Eleanor was furious. "Are you referring to my mother's mind?"

"No, the mind is an arbitrary thing. I am talking of the..."

"I know what you're talking about!" Eleanor screeched. "My mother's brain is in her head where it should be. In the ground. Buried in the holy ground."

"But what about the samples I took?"

"Are you completely without feeling? Are you utterly deranged? Why would you even commit such an atrocity? The good doctor had to put everything back and stitch and bandage her up as best he could so that she might have a little dignity in death."

Muriel put her hands to her face. No wonder she had felt so ill beside the grave. All her hard work thrown into the mouldering dirt. Not that it would be any use now, for if it had been two days or more since her grandmother had died, and her samples had not been preserved at the time, they would be of no use now. What a waste. When would she come across such a good case study again? The chances of finding such a brain and knowing years of the case history were impossible.

"I do not understand what has happened to you these past years," Eleanor continued. "I do not recognise you. You have treated me with contempt, disappearing for months, nay, it must be years at a time, with no word. You have refused to communicate with me. Then you appear here as if we are open to house you when you fancy, without a word of where you have been or what has happened. You are my child; I said I must tolerate this. But I will not tolerate such disrespect of the dead."

"I have never been disrespectful of a cadaver."

"Are you saying to me you have done this before?" Eleanor looked grey.

Muriel closed her eyes. Many people were uncomfortable with dissection and the meaning of it. How to make someone who knew nothing of the medical world understand? "When we die, the spirit is gone. There are only flesh and bones..."

"That was my mother. Your grandmother. You showed no respect. But you must be mad, or else why would you do it? I shall have to put you in an asylum."

Muriel felt her stomach drop like a rock. "No."

"Yes. I feel sick to look at you."

"Then I will leave."

"The doctor is keeping quiet on the understanding you will be locked away. As yet the truth hasn't gotten out into the town, but with time, something may slip out. It would destroy us. How could I and Jayne live here? And you'd be chased out with rocks and pitchforks."

"You and Jayne? She's no kin to you."

"Yes she is. I have told you."

"And you set preference to her over me? I am your daughter."

"I very much doubt that."

She felt tears prick at her eyes, then the flood started and Muriel slumped back into her chair. This had all come out of her control. All she had ever wanted to do was become a doctor, and she had shown them, although they could never see it, that a woman could become an authority in the medical profession. She had the mind and the ability. But society would not let her do it, her position as a female undermined it constantly. The child had almost destroyed everything and now when she tried to make advancements she was looked upon as a lunatic. People may find the anatomists disgusting, but on some level they understood it was all for the greater good of mankind. But that was when the men were working. When the woman worked, she was merely mad. "I am not mad and I am not a butcher," she wept.

Eleanor shrugged, calmed a little but still she could not bring herself to go to her daughter. "Yes, well, the doctor did say it looked like the work of a professional."

"I am a professional. I am a doctor."

"Don't talk such rot. You are not a doctor."

"I am! I am a highly respected anatomist in Edinburgh." She jumped out of her chair when her mother went to contradict her again. "I have written textbooks on the subject. I have studied at Edinburgh University. I am a doctor. You are just like every other fool, looking at me and seeing just another woman, as if that is all I am. I would have expected better of you. After all the things you have done in your life that people said you couldn't because you are just a woman. I am a doctor."

"But you can't be. They'd never let a woman study at the university."

"Yes, well," Muriel sat back down. "I may have dressed as a man when I was living up there. I may have used another name."

"And they believed you for a man."

"You just need confidence in yourself. Nolwenn helped me to play the part."

"Nolwenn?"

"Elizabeth's French maid."

"I should have known your sister would be involved in a reckless scheme like this."

"It was the only way. I don't have time to wait for generations to pass whilst they have the epiphany of what women can do. It's all I've ever wanted, and I've been wasting myself on all these other little endeavours all this time."

And so Muriel told her mother everything. Getting the clothes and learning the walk. Taking up a new name and moving to Edinburgh. Being accepted to study, finding lodgings, making great friends. Attending lectures and feeling her mind explode with possibility. She spoke of the terror of seeing a live operation, and the doubt that followed. Yet she had returned. She had a talent for the scalpel, and had turned to anatomy. The phrenologists all wanted one of her skulls, and she was researching the human body. There was great work being done, understanding how everything worked, how they could better treat maladies and help recovery when things broke down. It was an exciting time to be in the medical world.

"And the little girl?"

Muriel did not comprehend.

"Mairi."

"Elizabeth's daughter."

"Yes, but was she born of Elizabeth?"

Muriel would not meet her eye. She looked at the floor and did not speak.

Eleanor felt her heart break a little. Circumstance and single-minded drive had brought Muriel to this. She did not quite appreciate what she had sacrificed. "I cannot say I know much of medicine and so cannot make judgements on your capabilities as such. If you say you are a respected and talented anatomist then I will have to take your word for it."

Muriel looked up, hopeful for the first time.

"But you are not a good doctor."

"Mother, I..."

"No. A doctor is more than the knowledge in his head. He is about understanding the human condition and frailty. It is about having empathy with his fellow man."

"I have..."

"NO! You will not so much as acknowledge that little girl. And my mother was not even cold in her death bed when you started... that was my mother. Your grandmother. You did not have consent. You are no better than those grave robbers I read about. And I do not know if I can forgive you for these things."

"Mother, I was thinking of my work. The good we could do by studying the maladies of the mind..."

Eleanor waved the thought away like an annoying fly. "Your work is over."

"It has barely started."

"Do you remember nothing of what I said? If I don't do it, then the doctor will. He will speak. He will report everything to the authorities and then you will be taken away and thrown into prison or an asylum of their choosing or who knows what. The only option we have is where you are to be sent for your confinement."

"You can't lock me away."

"It is already done," Eleanor sighed. "I have already written to an asylum. The terms are agreed. They will come for you." It was a slight lie, for although letters had been sent, no terms had been settled on, but the details did not matter. Muriel had to understand that she had no control in the matter. She would be leaving Haworth and she would not be coming back.

"Mamma, you can't do this to me!"

"I have no choice. You mutilated my mother when she was just dead. And I have yet to hear an apology for the distress you have caused." She stood up. Judging by Muriel's face, this was the first time such a notion had even crossed her mind. So absorbed by her talent, her studies and her work, actual life and the worth of other living beings was lost to her. Eleanor walked to the door. "Given that you have disappeared for months, if not years, and all the things you have done, you cannot be trusted. I will have to keep you locked in here until they come for you."

"But, Mamma!"

"No. I am sorry it has come to this." Eleanor slipped through the door before Muriel could reach it, and quickly turned the lock. It was a new fitting that the blacksmith had arranged for her whilst Muriel had been incapacitated upstairs. Muriel would have to sleep in Maud's death bed for now. It would only be for a couple of days.

Muriel looked like a haggard wraith when they came. She had barely slept since she had been locked into the parlour. She'd listened to the movements of the house's day: Anne Thwaite arriving for work, little Jayne running about and chattering, asking why she couldn't go in the parlour, who was it that was in there. Muriel was taking rest as she was very ill and was not to be disturbed. The first time Eleanor brought food in, the opening of the door was very tentative, a long slow creak that grated against Muriel's loss of freedom. She would make no attempt at escape. Everything was finished. Her life was over, so she loitered in misery and did not touch the food she was given. Perhaps she could have starved herself to death, but for the arrival of the lunatic asylum's coach two days later.

She saw it from the parlour window, a dark, foreboding transportation with bars at the window, and three heavy, burly men sat outside. Presumably they were the coachman and two orderlies. Muriel was surprised they'd brought a coach with a full cover, rather than a ratty old farmer's cart. They could have trussed her up and slung her in the cart, for all the respect to her dignity she was about to receive, but then that would cause a scene and fuel for gossip for those who remained. It seemed Eleanor was concerned as to what might happen to Jayne.

Two of the men, the roughest of the three, jumped down and strode to the door and out of sight. There was some talk and Jayne was sent to her room, the patter of her childish footsteps running past the parlour door and up the staircase. She was irritated that she was not allowed to witness proceedings. Muriel remained on the edge of the bed and felt a little nauseous. Perhaps she should have eaten these past two days, kept her strength up and she might have been able to flee when the door was open and their guard was down.

The key turned in the lock.

Muriel began to weep, slow heavy tears for the end of the world.

The door opened and the men came inside without question or hesitation. Muriel's eyes widened in alarm as she saw the straight jacket one of them carried. "No!" she shrieked, scrabbling away into the back corner. She'd been to a lunatic asylum in Edinburgh once, and had seen the way those people were treated and the conditions they were kept in. If one wasn't mad when one went in, one certainly was when one left. Everything that she had worked for was about to be thrown into hell. Her mind, her ability, her knowledge, that one asset, had no value to any of the players now.

The man with the straight jacket gnashed his rotting teeth at her and shook the contraption at her. Muriel started to openly sob. Could her mamma not forgive her? Mamma, Mamma! Please don't do this.

"We have to bring that with us," the other man spoke. "Just in case, although we prefer not to. But we need folks to understand that they will not be running off. You'll be getting into that carriage and that's the end of it. We can tie you up in this, and don't think that we won't. Don't think that your women's tears will have any effect. I know from my bitter experience how deadly an insane woman can be."

"I'm not insane!"

He held up a hand. "Heard it all before. Now, you can get trussed up in this here if you like, or if you prefer, put a shawl about your shoulders and we'll walk out together all dignified and the like. You can show them that you have a little control over your actions, and we'll tell the doctor all about it. Put a good word in for you. Understand? Now, what's it to be?"

Muriel wiped at her eyes with the backs of her hands. She nodded and pulled her thickest shawl about her. When she stood up her legs almost gave way and she cried out, grasping the bedpost for support. The man with the straightjacket made a move as if she wasn't to be trusted, but his colleague stopped him with the slightest of glances. She straightened, and tried to stop crying and hold her head up. She must hold on to her own mind. It was all she had, and if she lost that then all was lost.

The corridor was empty and the door left wide open. Muriel went first and as they approached the door she felt one of the men grasp her arm, just to be sure she wouldn't make any silly attempts at escape. A solemn train, they moved through the garden and out to the dirt road where the carriage was waiting. Someone was inside, who unlatched the door and pushed it open. A dark cavern of ignorance awaited her. Muriel started crying again and felt her bladder go, the only consolation being that she was so dehydrated; there was barely any moisture within her to be expunged.

"Muriel!"

The three of them looked back to the house, where her mother stood in floods of tears, shrinking away into the mass of shawls she had clutched around her body. She did not look much better than Muriel. She was rapidly ageing from all the trauma of the past weeks. She lingered undecided for a moment before running across and grasping Muriel in a tight hug. She cradled the back of her daughter's head, felt the shuddering thin body and the loss of hope. "I'm sorry, Muriel, but you left me no choice," she cried. "You cannot stay here. And I may never see you again."

"Mamma! Mamma, please, don't do this."

"I must."

The orderlies pulled her off her mother and bundled her into the carriage, slamming the door shut. The vehicle shuddered and rocked as it swung around in a wide arc to start back the way it had come. Muriel flung herself to the barred windows, looking desperately to the bright light. She watched her distraught mother drop to the ground, a figure growing smaller and smaller as they moved away. She saw the doctor taking a walk, step up to the side of the road and give them a knowing nod as they passed. How could he be a part to this? If she'd been a man, he would have taken her actions as research; he would never have disregarded it as the lunacies of women.

Muriel clawed at the window, felt the bars shift under her hands, and wailed.

A cloth was thrown at her.

"Do calm down."

Muriel slumped into the seat, took the cloth without giving it much attention and wiped her face before blowing her nose. She crumpled the cloth into a messy ball and held it within her fist. She regarded the figure before her, caught in shadow and heavily dressed in overcoats and hats, scarves. It could have scarcely been human.

"I don't suppose there's any point in telling you I'm not mad."

The figure laughed.

On the outside they heard the men laugh amongst themselves. One spoke: "I hope to get a good tip after that performance."

Muriel scowled. "I wasn't that difficult. I've seen far worse patients, real lunatics, and how they writh..."

"Stop being so dramatic, Muriel," the figure scolded. The voice was clearer now, betraying its sex to be female. "He wasn't talking about your performance, rather his own."

"But I..."

The figure leaned forward to look out of the window. "I think we're safely away from the town now." Sitting back comfortably, hat and scarves were removed, and a playful face smiled back at her.

"Elizabeth," Muriel exclaimed. "I don't understand. Have you intercepted the asylum coach?"

Elizabeth rolled her eyes, already bored with Muriel's fantasies. "There never was one silly, this is all pretend. I've arranged it all with Mamma. We just had to get you out of the house in a suitably insane way to satisfy the doctor that Mamma was following his advice and you are off to be locked up. Honestly, Muriel, what were you thinking chopping up old Grannie's head? You could have at least waited until after the funeral."

"But Mamma was distraught."

"Of course she is. She may never see you again. Don't be naive. You're not going to an asylum, but you can never set foot in Haworth again. If the good doctor ever catches sight of you..."

"So what are you going to do with me?"

Elizabeth shrugged. "Take you to York. Pay off the actors, return the carriage. Beyond that I'm not quite sure. We'll plan that together. Perhaps in a couple of years we could say you've been cured in case you should ever see the doctor again, but it's probably best you don't return to Haworth. Nothing as nasty as gossip, or as long-lived as people's memories for the unseemly."

Muriel's hands shook. "So I'm not to be locked away?"

"Of course not, stupid. I thought you were supposed to be the clever one."

"But, I..." she looked to her hands and felt quite feint.

"Mamma said you weren't eating. I've got a basket with some treats here." She passed her younger sister the food. "And are you sorry now, for what you did to Mamma? Making her sad."

Muriel looked up from stuffing cheese into her mouth.

"Chopping up grannie."

"It was a dissection."

"I know, I know. Mamma can't quite believe how big you've become in the medical world. But you still shouldn't have done it. Are you not sorry at all?"

"Are you sorry?"

"For what?"

"Breaking Mamma's heart."

Elizabeth shuffled in her skirts and looked out of the window. "Yes, well. That was a long time ago. And one has to be free to live as one chooses." She looked back to Muriel. "Never mind. You eat your fill. And these two naughty girls will get themselves back to York. I think that's enough for now."

Emmerline's experience of her grandmother's death had been decidedly different. She had only ever briefly lived with the woman, a great many years ago. Beyond that period in her teenage years their relationship existed on sporadic visits infrequent letters. Maud had never been good with her letters, so it tended to be a one-sided conversation.

Due to family conflict that Emmerline had never completely understood, she had never seen any of her maternal aunts, cousins or grandparents whilst growing up. Her mother had kept her very separate from that part of the family. In fact, there was an aunt she had never met, for she had died before Emmerline's own mother's life had ended. When Clara had vaguely mentioned her sister Gillian, she had made a comment about a great brood of children. Most had been taken one winter with a fever, and the few that survived were nothing more than mere notions and concepts she rarely thought on.

Emmerline had received a note from Aunt Eleanor when Maud had died. A letter snuck through via the servants. Her husband had forbidden her to have anything to do with the family after the incident at Manchester, and just like a good girl, she had done as she was bade. Looking at her husband's drunken, angry face just now, she wasn't sure why she had ever listened to a word he said.

She had concocted a story about wanting to travel. Lying on the ground, she couldn't even remember what the lie had been, but the fact remained that she had managed to get away with a maid in a small gig, and attend her grandmother's funeral. She was confused that she felt no great sadness herself. Both Eleanor and Muriel looked like the worried dead, indeed Muriel looked as though she was coming down from a great intoxication. Grief could be consuming, yet it felt as though more than the simple death of an old lady was bothering the mother and daughter. The funeral had not the time to ask if there was anything she could do to help. She had been very conscious of the church full of curious locals, ears turned towards the wealthy lady attending. Whispers and glances fluttered around like fire. They would soon remember who she was and remarks would be made that she hadn't been seen here for a good time.

She paid her respects to Eleanor and Muriel without giving anything away, then went to stand in the background of the graveyard. She shuffled awkwardly, feeling the discomfort of a malicious gaze. She scanned across the crowds, but no one met her eye until she looked to the shade at the very far side where trees overhung the flat gravestones. In the middle of one such slab stood a short, gnarled old man with an oversized head for his body. He wore a nasty stare, old fashioned clothes but incredibly smart shoes and carried a knobbled walking stick.

I've seen you before, Emmerline thought.

Indeed you have my girl, his voice responded in her mind. I am your true grandfather. I stayed away as you asked, but now it is time for me to collect my wife.

She was another's wife.

I was first.

There was another before you.

They were never married. Besides, here she comes to me.

Indeed here came Maud. A young slip of a woman, flesh plump and unblemished, body toned from hard work but not even yet twenty. Her upper jaw was unbroken, not yet met with the hands of a blacksmith. Her hair was dark, long and sleek. She picked her way amongst the graves, heading towards that ugly old man. Emmerline wanted to cry. She did not think she had it in her to prevent this. What happened may well be for an eternity.

"That's right," the old man said, beckoning to her. "You are mine. Come here now."

Maud stopped a couple of meters away from him, outside of grasp, and looked about the churchyard. Don't do it, Emmerline pleaded silently. The young woman broke into a smile. The old hob almost rubbed his hands together in glee. Then Maud was skipping away towards the churchyard wall, and neither Emmerline nor the hob knew what had happened. There was a young, dark haired man standing in the road by the church, waving to Maud. She hurried through the gate and he took her hand before the two of them ran off towards the moors.

The hob glared at Emmerline. You did that, you witch.

I did nothing, she thought. Now, begone with you.

And he was gone.

She wished it was as easy to remove real living people from one's life. She looked to the ground in front of her, and focused on the fine details of the nearest plant. A hosta, she believed. She bent around the next kick and silently said her goodbyes. The little life growing inside her began to fade and within a minute it would be gone. Never to have been. I am so sorry you never had a chance.

If only he had gone for her face instead, the baby might have lived. But split lips and black eyes remained visible for days, if not weeks, and it would not do to have the staff gossiping. He had slapped her before, but nothing that would do more than a pink cheek that would quickly subside. She'd seen him this angry before, and this drunk, but never in combination. She closed her eyes as she felt the blood come between her legs.

Moses Whitfield leaned over his wife. She still had her eyes closed, but she could feel his hot breath, reeking of brandy. "You worthless little bitch," he snarled. A string of drool dangled before splattering her face. "You don't know what's good for you. If you ever disobey me again I will throw you out without a penny. You will never see your children again. I will pay you nothing. You can go rot in the poor house where you belong, guttertrash."

He stepped away from her to regain his composure, catch his breath and regain a respectable countenance. The couple were on top of a man made cliff, a tumble of rocks below with ferns and hostas carefully planted out. It had taken a year to construct, for Moses would keep changing his mind. He wanted it grander, grander, glorious to mark out his name and stand for all time. His poorly paid, overworked gardeners merely grunted and moved the boulder back to where it had originally stood.

Emmerline's eyes snapped open. She could see his feet shuffling as he straightened his cravat. A good portion of his wealth was her family money. And he was very correct in calling them 'her children' for beyond bothering her at night now and then, he had no input into those children whatsoever.

"Women are quite stupid. Like children. You do not learn from your mistakes. You should have learned your place and what is right after that embarrassment in Manchester. Your relatives are a disgrace. All these notions of workers having rights as if they were equals to us. Their betters. And yet you continue. You will not stop. I have been told about your visit to the mill. And talking to that man about the wool, trying to get us to buy it for worsted manufacture. What rot. What was his name? Salt? Who do you think you are talking to him about looking after staff better? Suggesting to a salesman that we aren't good employers. Bloody disgrace. And it's not like you have anything to do with business. Damned embarrassing. You make me regret the great favour in marrying you. You had that black mark over your head you know, your mother having killed your father. No one else would touch you."

Emmerline sat up. "There were several interested. They were just like you, interested in the money."

"Quiet, trollop. You have no money."

She stood up. Blood had soaked through the back of her skirts. It was in the earth where she had been. She could feel the cramps coming upon her. It was all over. She walked to her husband.

He was still waffling. "By god, when I think of all the good deeds I have done for you. The good home I have created for our children. And I found those letters and plans. Who do you think you are, writing to architects? Build a village for the workers to live in? They already have homes."

"They live in squalor."

"Nonsense. They are used to it. Give them mansions to live in and you will never get a good days work out of them. Do you see me giving my horses parlours and sitting rooms? A good day's work is what keeps their souls going."

He turned to face her as she approached. It looked as though the fury had subsided, although the drunkenness and the contempt was still present. "Dear God, Emmerline, you really are pathetic. If it wasn't for me..."

"I've had just about enough of this."

Moses chortled at her. She looked like a high class trollop, in her fine but dirtied and torn dress, her hair pulled out of style with leaves and small twigs caught within the strands. "You'll take what your husband gives you and you'll be quiet about it."

"You remind me of a man I once knew."

He sneered at her. "Do be quiet, Emmerline, I'm quite bored of you." He moved to walk away, but his feet staggered in the dry gravel as he realised he was right at the edge of the artificial cliff edge. He wobbled drunkenly, and would have regained his balance, if it wasn't for the smart, hard shove in the small of his back. He wobbled for a moment before his feet pattered as if on ice and he went over the edge. There was a crunch as his neck was broken. His body twisted ungainly against one of the boulders. A moist crack echoed off the landscaping. Moses' body spread as he landed, a rock cracking his skull open. Blood bloomed out against the garden.

She stood at the top of the cliff and regarded him coolly. Enough was most definitely enough. Trying to ignore the cramps, she calmly walked back to the house, taking care to follow the smaller tracks and avoid the gardening gangs. Upon reaching the lawn, she lay on one of the seats long enough to stain it with blood before rushing inside and crying for help with her baby. Staff got her to bed and sent for the doctor. The dead, tiny baby was born before the doctor arrived. Emmerline was cleaned up and put into fresh bedding, given a tincture so that she might sleep. The doctor walked down with the housekeeper, arriving at the ground floor just as one of the gardeners rushed in, having forgotten himself. They'd just found the master, dead in the garden. It looked as though he had tripped and fallen over the cliff. Would the doctor kindly come and help them?

Emmerline paused in the reception hall as she caught sight of herself in the grand mirror. What a miserable black dress. She still had another year to wear these horrible clothes before she was free. There were so many social rules for a widow, it was just further punishment. All for pushing a husband over a cliff. There had been no fuss the first time she'd dealt with an unwanted man by a cliff. Still, she ought to be thankful that no one had ever been in the slightest suspicious.

In some ways it was a shame her children would not grow up to better know their father, for she had wanted Lydia and Charity to see what to avoid, and Mowbray what not to become. Life lessons were one thing but they could not have continued living under such a buffoon. Especially after he had killed her fourth child. No one ever mentioned that. No one knew that he had kicked the child out of her. But even the miscarriage was never alluded to. Such embarrassing women's things were to be hushed and ignored. Look to the other side of the room and wait until it has left by the servant's entrance.

Two years of pretending. She didn't miss the social engagements, and was much occupied in spending more time with her children and working on the construction of her new workers' village. She'd taken a hand in the running of the mills, and immediately stopped all children under ten working. It was a ruling which had resulted in plenty of complaints from families who needed the wage. Some had even left to work at other mills. Emmerline was horrified they could value their children so little, but then she had seen the accounts, and what these people had to live off. She raised the wages to cover the loss and looked forward to getting people into her village houses, their children into the little school, and all living in healthy air with good sanitation. It was a great thing that she was about to achieve in her husband's memory.

She smiled as she sauntered back to the drawing room. Some of his cronies had been dumbfounded when she had said this was his dream. They knew how he scorned the common man. He'd wanted to better the lives of others? What rot. This is what happened when a woman was put in charge. Emmerline needed marrying off before she did anything stupid. Think of how those children will be raised now. A couple of eligible bachelors raised their suite, but Emmerline coyly pulled her black veil over her face and feigned horror. It was not even two years since her husband had died.

"Well, has little Mowbray calmed down now that his dear mamma has kissed his little forehead goodnight."

"Elizabeth," Muriel scolded, "You can't be a guest and sarcastic."

Elizabeth burst out into a gleeful laugh and waved her ostrich feather fan in front of her as if trying to start a fire. "This is hardly being out in society. It's just family here."

"I don't think your gown knows that."

"Hush now, you're only jealous. Even my skinny sister wouldn't get her waist into this dress."

"No one would get into that dress." Emmerline stood at the back of the room and regarded the two sisters. This was only the second time she had met the fabled Elizabeth MacCaskill, mother of Mairi, wealthy society courtesan and beauty of an impossibly narrow waist. The engineering that must go on under that gown could not be good for a person's constitution. But she did look stunning, full of life and thrilled with every moment. Perhaps a life of immorality was the way. Elizabeth had turned forty this year, still no white hairs to be seen, instead her dark hair rich and luxurious, the jewel decorations in her hair glinting in candlelight. There was a heavy necklace about her neck, her lower cut dress – very French, don't you know – was a heavy dark satin. Very suitable for mourning, but Elizabeth made it look decadent. And now that the rash across her back had cleared up, it was the moment to whip this dress out.

It was quite shocking she had such a woman in her house, but this was just a family affair, the three cousins gathering. The servants wouldn't know who she was, and given the maid's surly French response, no gossip would get out about the hall.

"You ought to let him cry a little," Elizabeth said. "Nip it in the bud, before he grows up to be another troublesome man."

"Isn't that what all men are?" Emmerline pondered as she walked around to the cluster of armchairs and seating by the fire.

"I don't think any of us have had any luck with men," Muriel muttered, staring to the flames.

Emmerline raised her eyebrows as if to say, what men do you know? She caught Elizabeth's canny stare. She sensed there was a lot she didn't know.

"Just think of our grandfather. You can trace the rot back to there."

"Surely you're not suggesting that all the men in our family are rotten? Please don't sully our brother's memory." Elizabeth said. "And I'm sure from what little I remember Mamma saying, our Uncle Stephen was a very decent fellow."

"My father was a good man," Emmerline interjected.

"Until your mother poisoned him."

"She did not poison him."

"They hung her for it."

Emmerline met Elizabeth's bold eye. She'd never met anyone quite like her. No one in polite society would be so abrupt and callous to her face. Elizabeth wouldn't know about polite society and how to behave. It was not something she had been exposed to. She walked on the edge, providing the fantasy play world for the men who could afford it.

"She was innocent of that crime. Some old fraudster had tried to poison my mother. Mamma knew too much about herbs, poisons, to be caught out. But my father must have taken it accidentally."

Elizabeth didn't look convinced, but didn't press it any further. Silence spoke more.

"I think we can safely say we've all failed at partnership, at relationships." Muriel said, to draw the women away from a pending argument.

"Speak for yourself!" Elizabeth laughed. "I get along very well with men."

"Only as long as they have amusement and a use of you." Emmerline said.

"I'm not an idiot, I have my securities, and my own wealth in my own name. I am not as dependent on them as you might think."

"I was really referring to the traditional state of affairs: marriage," Muriel said. "The ideal ending that we are all to aspire to. Living happily together until death do us part."

"I've never heard of such a thing in real life." Elizabeth scoffed.

"Yes well. I do think we cousins have had particular bad luck in our choices and circumstances." Now and then she still wondered about Erskine, married to someone else, probably with children by now, up in the highlands of Scotland. Did he ever wonder about her, Kaarel Must's true self?

"We can hope our children have better luck."

"I'm a widow. I don't suppose I'm allowed to own this, but I don't miss him."

"I'm glad to hear it," Elizabeth said. "I never met him, but I heard plenty. You know he had a woman installed in..."

"Elizabeth!" Muriel shrieked. "Emmerline doesn't need to know."

Emmerline shrugged. "I had an inkling."

"If it's any consolation, most of the rich ones have another woman. They pay for the apartment, the clothes, the upkeep. They'd all deny it in polite society of course, as though immorality is only in the pages of novels and criminal minds..."

Elizabeth's speech was interrupted by a knock, then the entrance of one of Emmerline's servants. He walked across the room in a manner that didn't seem to part the air nor touch the rugs with his feet. He stopped by Emmerline's side and bent forward to impart a message.

Emmerline's brow creased in confusion. "She's here now? To see me? I don't understand it. I haven't seen the woman for years."

"She says the post broke down just outside the village..."

"I'm sure the village could have looked after her."

"Shall I arrange transportation back..."

"No, no," Emmerline shook her head in exasperation. "Let her come in. And have a room made up. We must remember our manners."

"Very good, ma'am."

"Are we to get a surprise guest?" Elizabeth, sprawled out on a camelback sofa as the only occupant, sat up and leaned forward. "I thought this was just to be an intimate evening of cousins."

"So did I but it seems the post carriage broke down close by. Everyone else returned to the village, but Anne Lister decided she'd come up to the hall. I've not seen the woman for years. Not since my departed spouse had those dinner parties, do you remember, Muriel?"

"I do. I wonder why she'd coming back now? Perhaps the thought of village digs were too basic for her."

"Maybe she's coming to court your fortune!" Elizabeth laughed.

"She has her own hall," Muriel said. "Her uncle died a few months ago, left her Shibden Hall."

"How the news gets down to Pateley Bridge! I would have thought a surgeon would be too busy to listen to society gossip." Elizabeth declared.

"I am only a surgeon's assistant."

"I think it's wonderful you have any title of your own from your own merit," Emmerline spoke. "Besides," she added, looking to Elizabeth, "Your little joke may have a grain of truth. There are rumours about Miss Lister. Her heart is only true to ladies."

"Really?" Elizabeth's eyebrows shot up. "This woman I have to meet."

Muriel looked to the fire whilst her cousins swapped gossip. Anne Lister and gossip in Pateley Bridge aside, it was good to finally be recognised for something and in her own identity. It was a far cry from what she was capable of, or what people would ever trust her to do. After a couple of months missing from the public's eye (hidden in Elizabeth's apartments), Muriel took on a slightly new identity, as Muriel Must, the recently widowed tragedy, abandoned by the disease that had taken her dear husband, Kaarel Must. He had been her guide in life, and had taken it upon himself to train her in all medical practices. They had hoped to bring medical enlightenment out into the very wildernesses, and he had felt a wife needed to be equally qualified. In fact, before his death he had even written to some of his Edinburgh colleagues about his latest experiment. They all wrote back declaring him quite mad, and to desist in such a waste of time. A woman could never understand the complexities of the human body. Elizabeth had laughed like a witch when she had read that line. Still, Kaarel insisted his work was exceeding expectation. But before he could write any more, a terrible sweating illness came upon him and he died. It was left to his widow to write to all of his learned acquaintances and tell them the terrible news. In her new identity, Muriel received many letters and cards of condolences, including a strange, short note that mentioned the good doctor Erskine MacKenzie and how he had received the news. She puzzled and waited, surely to God he would understand what this meant, and who the grieving widow Muriel Must actually was. She fooled herself he would come, but she never heard a word.

So she had written to the surgeon in Pateley Bridge where Kaarel had planned to go and work. The surgeon looked after the town's health, including doctoring and some apothecary work. Kaarel had wished to research and learn about the drugs and tinctures. Circumstances had changed drastically, and although the exact nature of his planned research would be changed, she had a proposition for them. She found herself without a regular source of income, but having studied under her husband, felt she had something to offer society and was keen to learn. It was extremely unorthodox, and at first the man had been uninterested and a little shocked by the idea, but after some correspondence, began to come around to the idea. Having a woman there may help with some of the female patients and their particular ailments. They could test it on a trial basis and take things from there.

The door opened, interrupting her reflections. "Miss Anne Lister," the servant announced, and Anne Lister, a statement in black, came striding across the room to Emmerline.

"Mrs Whitfield," Anne came up to her. "Thank you for attending to me in my hour of need. The post broke down and there were so many of us, and such a little village..."

"Miss Lister, do not worry," Emmerline smiled politely and waved a hand around the empty chairs by the fire. "It has been a long time since you were last here, but I cannot turn away a soul in need. Please sit. We'll have refreshments shortly."

Anne straightened and looked about her, realising for the first time that Emmerline had company. "Miss MacCaskill, how very nice to see you again," she greeted Muriel. "It has been a long time since I saw you about Halifax with those textbooks. It's as if you simply disappeared."

"I am in Pateley Bridge now. Working." Ah, trade, Muriel saw the look cross Anne's face. Rumours about women were one thing, but Anne's bias towards the rich being a better stock of person were more of known fact. All considered it was surprising she would come to Emmerline. Rich yes, but the widow of a manufacturing family. Anne liked nobility and the landed gentry. Still, if the post had broken down, needs must. "You won't have met my sister, Elizabeth MacCaskill."

Anne shifted on her heel and her eyes lit up. "I certainly have not. I would remember such a meeting." She walked over to Elizabeth, who was smiling and flashing her eyes behind her fan, and sat down next to her. "Why on earth have we never had you in Halifax society?"

Elizabeth shook her head and laughed. "I don't really do society. My goodness, Anne, the things I've heard about you. Surely not so naive."

Muriel held her breath, expecting a snobbish reaction or retort, but instead Anne looked captivated, and the two women started their conversational dance. Muriel lent across to her cousin, balancing her elbow on the arm of Emmerline's chair so that she might stretch to her cousin's ear. "By god," she whispered. "I do believe she's seducing her."

Emmerline pursed her lips and met Muriel's eye. "Yes, but I wonder which one you mean."

Historical Note

This is a work of fiction. The characters and stories are fiction and a work of the author's imagination. However, a number of characters are based on actual historical figures, appearing as highly fictionalised versions of themselves. Furthermore, events such as the Peterloo Massacre in Manchester, really did occur, and any errors in the portrayal are entirely the author's.

The Bronte family hardly need any introduction for they are so internationally well-known. Their father, Patrick Bronte came to work at Haworth after some local politics over who would succeed the deceased Mr Charnock. For the time period this book covers, the Bronte children were just that: children. They lived in Haworth, the older girls were sent away to a boarding school, where the two eldest sisters tragically became terminally ill. The Crow Hill bog burst did actually happen, and the children had been out walking that way on the day.

Anne Lister, born of Market Weighton, and eventually to be owner of Shibden Hall just outside of Halifax was another true life contemporary. She was a known eccentric who never married, and loved the fairer sex. She wore dark clothing, ran her estates, when inherited, herself and on her own terms and was a great traveller and an inquisitive mind. She was also an obsessive diarist, often writing in code, which is how we come to know now so much about her life.

In the medical world the Phrenology Society, and indeed phrenology itself was all the rage. People believed a person's character and abilities could be read from the shape of the skull. John Snow and James Simpson were only children at the time of this story. John Snow was born in York and later ended up in London working as a pioneering doctor. James Simpson, who studied in Edinburgh, worked with chloroform and brought this as an anaesthetic to the operating room.